Zoey was trembling, big violent spasms that shook her whole body and made her teeth chatter.

Mr. Ruggles's words echoed in her brain . . . *You realize that there's a lot of things you want to put right . . . a lot of folks you ought to forgive for old wrongs . . . and tell them that you love them, and there's just no more time . . .*

Zoey thought about her ferry ride with Adam last night and how magical it had seemed, but how it was now tarnishing in front of her eyes. Because if she were dying, would she think of Adam?

She closed her eyes. No, she would think of Lucas and this smelly fishing boat and her unwashed hair and how none of it mattered, none of it mattered in the slightest; the only thing that mattered, the only thing that she had ever cared about, that had ever made her happy—

"Oh, Lucas!" she wailed . . .

Don't miss any of the books in
Making Out
by Katherine Applegate
From Avon Books

MAKING OUT #28

Zoey comes home

KATHERINE APPLEGATE

AVON BOOKS

An Imprint of HarperCollinsPublishers

Library of Congress Catalog Card Number: 99-69744
ISBN: 0-380-81532-X

First Avon edition, 2000

AVON TRADEMARK REG. U.S. PAT. OFF. AND IN OTHER COUNTRIES,
MARCA REGISTRADA, HECHO EN U.S.A.

Zoey comes home

Zoey

You know the problem with writing about being angry and hurt and betrayed by Lucas and Nina? I'm sick of it. At this point it just makes me tired.

But I guess I can't stop writing about it until I stop feeling angry and hurt and betrayed.

How long do I have to go on feeling this way? Shouldn't some internal defense mechanism be acting up about now? Shouldn't my body be deciding that it's had enough of feeling terrible and decide that one of these mornings I'm going to wake up happy?

1

Sometimes, of course, I do wake up happy, for a moment or two. And then I think, "What was it I had to feel horrible about?" and then I remember. And that part, the remembering, never gets any better. It's always as painful as the first time I imagined Nina and Lucas kissing.

Claire

I remember once about a year ago, we were all sitting around a table in the high school cafeteria and Zoey asked us, very seriously, if we thought there was a difference between like and love. As in, if you were in love with someone, did that mean you just liked them a whole lot? Or was love something altogether different?

Lately I've been thinking about that a lot. For instance, last night Paolo said something that made me so angry I was literally spitting, and then he laughed and said that he didn't mean it, that he only likes to make me angry because my chest heaves.

And I wondered (maybe I
should ask Zoey?) if it's possible
to be in love with someone you
don't even _like._

Nina

I don't know why this never occurred to me before, but I suddenly realized that the Passmores, as a family, in their entirety, can't stand me.

Zoey hates me because I'm her ex-best friend, Benjamin doesn't want to be near me because I'm his ex-girlfriend, Mr. Passmore never liked me because I broke his turkey platter when I was seven and he never really got over it, and Mrs. Passmore must think I'm basically just kinda pathetic.

Boy, I wonder if when they see me coming, they're all

just like, "Gross. You talk to her." "No, you talk to her." "No, you do it."

Well, frankly, that's a pretty upsetting thought because of the four Passmores, I like two of them and I love two of them, and it's a little disturbing to think that none of them likes me back.

I guess it goes without saying which two I love.

Aisha

For the longest time my little brother, Kalif, went around telling these really revolting jokes. They all went something like this:

Question: What's worse than catching a baby falling from a helicopter?
Answer: Catching it on the first bounce!

And a whole lot of other jokes that don't really bear repeating and weren't even funny to begin with, just nauseating.

But for some crazy reason, lately I've been wanting to think up my own joke. The question part would go like this:

What's worse than walking into your dorm room with your boyfriend and seeing your gorgeous roommate wearing nothing more than a baby doll nightgown?

But I can't decide what the answer would be. Having your boyfriend whistle? Having your boyfriend drool?

Or this: Standing behind your boyfriend and not being able to see his face?

One

Zoey dumped the last bag of groceries in the back of the van and checked her list. Supermarket, butcher shop, bakery, pharmacy . . . Yes, she was finally done shopping.

She slammed the door of the van and groaned. If only Mrs. Gray hadn't asked Zoey to run errands this morning while Benjamin went over the books with her father at the restaurant. All Zoey had wanted to do was take a hot bath and sort through the clothes that had finally arrived from California. She had wanted to find something simple but flattering to wear when she met their cousin Adam, who was arriving today. But how could she refuse Mrs. Gray? She was giving them free room and board, after all.

Zoey sighed and walked around the van, glancing at herself in the driver's-side mirror. So now instead of looking elegant and pulled together, she looked pale and washed-out, without makeup, her hair pulled back in a ponytail that emphasized her heart-shaped face. Her nostrils were still pink from a cold she'd had last week, and Zoey thought she looked kind of rabbity.

She climbed into the van and started the engine. She didn't know why she wanted to look nice in order to meet Adam, who was her cousin, after all, although of the second or third variety and adopted. Hardly a close blood tie. She supposed it was because of the way he had sounded on the phone last night, so cool and easygoing and dependable. He'd said that he would arrive on an early flight and take the 10 A.M. ferry. When Zoey had hesitantly explained that she wasn't sure where he would stay, he'd laughed and said that he was bringing a folding bed and he would sleep in the back room of the restaurant.

Zoey winced a little at the thought. Imagine sleeping in the restaurant. She already felt as though she spent twenty-four hours a day there. But Adam had sounded cheerful and confident. "Don't worry about a thing," he'd said to Zoey, and the words were like music to her ears. Finally someone was telling her not to worry, that he would take care of things. Someone she could truly rely on, not like Lucas, who promised the world and then jerked it away from you at the last second—

I will not think about Lucas, Zoey resolved for about the millionth time.

She put the van in reverse and was backing out of her parking space when a sign in the window of the Historical Society caught her eye.

LOCAL WRITER WANTED
TO COMPOSE DEDICATION FOR
THE *CAROLINA* SHIPWRECK
50TH ANNIVERSARY EXHIBITION

Zoey sighed again. The words *local writer* always stirred a daydream deep within her. She fantasized constantly about returning to Chatham Island as a successful author and having a book signing in the Weymouth bookstore. People would line up for her autograph and Lucas would hear about it and—

"God, enough with the Lucas revenge fantasies," she said out loud.

She pulled out of the parking lot and glanced at her watch. If she hurried, she could catch the 12:30 ferry.

Her foot pressed down harder on the accelerator as she raced through the business district of Weymouth. Now, if only she could make this last light and find a decent parking spot—

A flashing blue light in the rearview mirror made her roll her head slowly as though someone had hit her. *Damn it!*

She pulled over to the side of the road and stopped the van. In her mirror she could see the police officer climbing out of his patrol car. Zoey took a deep breath and hoped he liked rabbits.

Claire Geiger walked along the MIT campus, wondering why every guy in the world seemed to interpret the wearing of a miniskirt as an invitation to run his eyes all over her body. She wasn't wearing this red suede miniskirt for them; she was wearing it for herself. She liked the way she looked in the miniskirt, with a white blouse, black tights, and a black wool jacket. Her dark hair fell in rich waves to below her shoulder blades, and her brown eyes sparkled in her fine-featured face.

"Hello, Claire," a voice said, interrupting her thoughts.

She looked up. "Hi, Paolo."

He fell into step beside her. "It's always so nice to see a girl walking along, thinking about what a pretty picture she makes."

She frowned at him in irritation. "Don't let me keep you from wherever you were going."

He smiled. "Why do you always get so mad when I tell the truth about something?"

"Because you always twist things around and—oh, I don't know," Claire said, giving up. She laughed. "Besides, *don't* I look pretty?" She spun around in a circle.

"Yes, you look very pretty," Paolo said, and though his smile was mocking, his eyes were appreciative. "Now, stop preening, Claire, and come have a cup of coffee with me. I just have time before my next class."

He didn't ask me if I have time, Claire thought. *Or even if I want to go! He's so nervy.*

But she didn't resist when Paolo grabbed her hand and began leading her toward the student union.

"God, I just finished tutoring this girl who is such a birdbrain," Paolo said. "She actually thought Frank Lloyd Wright was one of the Wright brothers. Unbelievable."

"I thought you tutored Spanish," Claire said. "How did Frank Lloyd Wright come up?"

"I read her history paper as a special favor," Paolo said.

A fingernail of jealousy scraped at Claire's heart. Why was he doing special favors for this girl? Did she have a great smile? Beautiful legs? A perfect figure?

"What was she . . . like?" Claire asked.

"Who?"

"The girl you were tutoring."

He glanced at her and grinned. "Don't worry, she wasn't pretty."

Claire flushed. "That wasn't what I asked!"

"But that's what you meant."

"It is not!"

"Oh?" He made his face blank. "What did you want to know about her, then?"

"Well . . . is she a freshman?" Claire asked, a bit flustered.

"Yes, and she'll never get to be a sophomore, believe me," Paolo said. He ruffled her hair. "And she's not one-tenth as gorgeous as you, and she doesn't have eyebrows that draw together when I tease her or an incredible smile, and you have nothing to worry about. Now, come on."

He turned toward the glass doors of the union, but a guy in a green T-shirt with Safe Sex Week stenciled on it stopped him. "Free condom?" he asked, holding out a foil-wrapped square. "It's National Safe Sex Week."

"Sure," Paolo said, taking the condom. "Thanks."

"How about you?" the guy said, holding one out to Claire.

"We're together," Paolo said to the guy. "She's the one I'm going to *use* the condom with."

"Paolo!" Claire said.

"What?"

Claire bit her lip. She was too embarrassed to say, *"We don't have sex!"* and she figured *"We're barely*

13

even dating!" would sound even worse, so she just gestured to the guy in the T-shirt and said, "I'm sure he's not interested in all the details."

"Of course he is," Paolo said, looking surprised. He turned to the guy. "Aren't you?"

The guy grinned. "Sure."

"See?" Paolo said to Claire. "He's very interested!" He spoke to the guy again. "What else can I tell you?"

"Paolo!" Claire said again, yanking him away by the hand.

"What?" he asked, stumbling after her.

"You're embarrassing me!"

"Why?" he asked innocently, leaning across her to stuff the condom into her purse.

"You know why," Claire said. "I don't want to talk about it."

"Talk about what?" Paolo said. "Our sex life?"

"We don't have a sex life!" Claire practically shouted.

"Well, no need to get so upset about it," Paolo said. "We can fix that right away. You busy tonight?"

Claire rolled her eyes. "I refuse to discuss this anymore. Besides, I have to be in class in about ten minutes."

"Meaning what? That ten minutes isn't long enough to do it?"

"Paolo!" She blushed again. "No, meaning, I have to get going."

"Okay," Paolo said, pulling some change out of his pocket. "Let me get some coffee. Want anything?"

"No, thanks." She followed him to the vending machine.

Paolo pressed the buttons, and the vending machine hissed and began filling a paper cup with black coffee. "So what are we doing this weekend?"

Is that his way of asking me out? Claire thought irritably.

"I don't know what *you're* doing," she said, "but *I'm* going to a climatology conference."

There, she thought. *That will teach him to wait until Thursday to ask about the weekend.*

"Climatology conference?" Paolo asked. "When did you decide to go to that?"

About five seconds ago, Claire thought. But she only said lightly, "I signed up for it at the beginning of the year. All the climatology students are going. It's a sort of weekend retreat."

"Where is it?" Paolo asked.

"Princeton."

"You're kidding!" Paolo said. "Princeton, New Jersey?"

"Yes, of course."

"Well, that's perfect," Paolo said, removing the paper cup from the vending machine. "Princeton is my hometown. I can drive you to the conference, and then you and I can both stay at my parents' house."

"I am not staying at your parents' house," Claire said, pushing open the glass doors.

Good Lord, she thought. *A whole household of Paolos! I'd lose my mind.*

"Come on, it'll be a blast," Paolo said.

"No," Claire said. "Nay. Nix. Negative."

15

Paolo grabbed her hand again. "Hey," he called to the safe sex guy. "Can we have a few more condoms? Because I'm taking Claire home to meet my parents, and you know what a turn-on *that* is."

Two

Aisha sat at a table in the student cafeteria, trying to
write a letter to Christopher and wondering why she
always got a run in her tights. Here she was, wearing a gray flannel skirt and red sweater set, with her
curly hair pulled back in a clip, doing her best to
look like a pretty Harvard college girl, and the
whole effect was ruined by a big stupid run in her
black tights.

She tucked the leg with the run under her and
turned back to her letter. She hadn't gotten very far.

Dear Christopher,
    *I'm so sorry I ruined last
weekend for us. I know it was
all my fault. It's just that I
hate sharing you, and when you
invited Felicia along with us, I
felt so*

What was she going to write next? *I felt so threatened and insecure, I thought I was going to start*

17

crying? That I couldn't shake the horrible feeling that if I disappeared, the two of you wouldn't have cared?

Aisha sighed. And saying that it was all her fault rankled, too. Why *had* Christopher invited Felicia along? Didn't he want to be alone with Aisha, especially now when they hardly ever had the chance?

Aisha turned to a fresh page in her notebook and wrote *Dear Christopher* on the top line with determination. But then a flash of color caught her eye, and she looked up.

It was Felicia, striding across the cafeteria toward a group of her friends. Felicia wore bootleg jeans, a lime green sweater, and a thrift shop fur jacket. Her heavy blond hair hung halfway down her back. Aisha felt jealousy well up in her like a poisonous liquid. If Aisha wore that outfit, she would look like a clown. But Felicia didn't; Felicia looked sexy. Suddenly Aisha felt like more of a frump than ever.

And now she was going to have to sit here by herself while Felicia lounged at another table, surrounded by admirers. Maybe she should gather up her stuff and go study at the library or something—

"Well, if it isn't Aisha Gray," a voice said from behind her. "Just the person I've been trying to spontaneously bump into for weeks."

Aisha looked up, grateful to whoever sounded so happy to see her. Then she blinked in surprise. "Graham?"

"None other," Graham Stevenson said, sliding into a chair next to her. Aisha had met him on a bus last summer, before she even knew she would be coming to Harvard.

She smiled. "I'm surprised you recognized me," she said.

"Oh, I never forget pretty girls," he said lightly, and Aisha warmed to the compliment. At least there was one guy in Cambridge who wasn't falling at Felicia's feet.

"So," she said, "how's your life been since August?"

He shrugged. "Busy. But fun. And you? How's it going with the on-again, off-again fiancé?"

"Oh, it's on again, very much so," Aisha said, twisting her silver engagement ring absently.

"Is that the guy I saw you with last weekend?" Graham asked.

She nodded in surprise. "Where did you see us? Why didn't you say hello?"

Graham smiled. "I didn't know if he was the jealous type."

No, that's me, Aisha thought. But she looked at Graham wryly and said, "He has nothing to be jealous of, right? We only sat by each other on a bus."

"Yeah, but guys know," Graham said. "He'd take one look at me and know that I spent the whole bus ride imagining you and me—"

"Graham, stop it!" But Aisha couldn't help laughing.

He smiled at her. "Seriously, I wanted to ask you if you and hubby—"

"His name is Christopher."

"If you and Christopher would like to go on a double date with me and my girlfriend next time Christopher's in town," Graham said.

"You have a girlfriend?" Aisha said skeptically. "What about the famous bus ride that broke your heart?"

"I'm a quick healer," he said, grinning. "Besides, she hasn't been my girlfriend for very long."

"That would be great," Aisha said, realizing how much she meant it. How nice it would be to have a friend, a real friend, at Harvard. "Christopher should be in town this weekend or next."

"Great," Graham said. "Will you call me?"

"Sure . . . Oh, wait, write down your number," Aisha said. She handed him her notebook, and he scribbled down his number.

"You know, you can call me for coffee or something, too," he said. "Just as friends."

Aisha looked at his steady blue eyes. "I'd like that."

"Good," Graham said. He stood up. "Now I have to go to class."

"Oh, me too," Aisha said. "Let me walk with you."

She shoved her books and notebooks in her bag quickly, her spirits lifting. Maybe now every single time the phone rang, it wouldn't be for Felicia. And when Christopher came to visit, she could take him out with her friends—

Aisha frowned suddenly. Why was it that she didn't mind sharing Christopher with Graham when she had resented it so fiercely with Felicia? Could it be because Graham didn't threaten her—and Felicia did?

But Aisha didn't want to think about it, so she brushed the thought from her mind and hurried to catch up to Graham.

The guy sitting at a table with Benjamin and Christopher in the empty restaurant was tall and broad shouldered, with hazel eyes and a pleasant, square-jawed face. He rose to his feet as soon as Zoey entered.

"You must be Zoey," the guy said, holding out his hand. "I'm Adam."

Zoey flushed with embarrassment. She had never felt more flustered or rumpled in her life. She shook his hand and said hastily, "I'm so sorry I'm late. I've had the worst morning."

They both sat down at the table, and Zoey saw that they had all the account books out.

"What happened?" Benjamin asked.

Zoey bit her lip. "Where's Dad?"

"He got tired and went to lie down," Benjamin said. "Why?"

"I got a speeding ticket!" Zoey said. "It was so aggravating—"

"How fast were you going?" Benjamin interrupted.

"Sixty."

"That doesn't sound so bad," Adam said mildly.

Zoey felt sheepish. "Well, it was in a thirty-mile-an-hour zone."

Benjamin and Christopher moaned in unison.

"Oh, my God," Benjamin said.

"It wasn't completely my fault," Zoey protested. "You know how the van speedometer just has those dots? And not numbers?"

Benjamin and Christopher snickered.

"Did you tell that to the policeman?" Christopher asked.

"Well, yes," Zoey said.

Benjamin and Christopher laughed harder at this.

She made a face. "He wasn't very sympathetic, either."

"How much was the ticket?" Adam asked.

"It was going to be four hundred dollars—" Zoey started.

"Four hundred dollars!" Benjamin moaned again and covered his eyes. "Jesus, Zoey."

"I said, it was *going to be* four hundred," Zoey said. "But I talked him out of it."

Benjamin uncovered one eye. "You did? What do you have to do, marry him?"

"No," Zoey said indignantly. "All I have to do is go to driving school."

Benjamin and Christopher began laughing again.

"Will you guys please quit that?" she asked in annoyance.

"I can't help it," Christopher said. "It just gets better and better."

"What's so hilarious about me going to driving school?" Zoey demanded. "It's only three lessons."

"Yeah, and maybe they can teach you to read speedometers with *dots*," Benjamin said.

Zoey rolled her eyes and then smiled at Adam. "You'll have to forgive these two. Their senses of humor are still stuck at about the ten-year-old level. Have they even given you a tour yet? Have you unpacked? Are you hungry? Anything?"

Adam smiled. "Yes, they've given me the tour, and we've even gone over the accounts. Benjamin was just about to take me up to the Grays'."

"Mrs. Gray says Adam can put his bed in one of their dressing rooms," Christopher said.

"Oh, that's wonderful!" Zoey said. "I couldn't bear to think of anyone sleeping in that back room. You'd probably have recurring nightmares about the chicken special within a week."

Adam's hazel eyes were amused. "Well, Mrs. Gray has saved me from that."

"Why don't you take Adam up to the B&B?" Benjamin said. "I have to set up for lunch, anyway."

"Sure," Zoey said. She turned to Adam. "Do you have a suitcase?"

"Right here," he said, picking up a small duffel bag.

Zoey stood up. "I'll be back as soon as I show Adam around and take a shower," she said to Benjamin.

She led Adam outside. He walked next to her, swinging the duffel bag lightly.

Zoey pushed her damp bangs off her forehead. "I don't know if Benjamin already told you this," she said. "But we're just astronomically grateful to you. You don't know how much we need the help to keep the restaurant going. Dad still gets tired so easily."

Adam smiled. "You don't have to be astronomically grateful, Zoey. Or even cosmically. I was glad to come when your dad called. It solved a couple of problems at home."

"Really?" Zoey said, curious. "Like what?" Suddenly she was embarrassed. "If you don't mind my asking."

Adam shook his head. "I don't mind at all. It's no big deal. I'm just taking the semester off law school, and my mother sort of flips out whenever she thinks about it."

"Why did you take the semester off?" Zoey asked.

"I'm just not sure I want to be a lawyer," Adam said, shrugging. "And I'd just as soon figure that out before I get all the way through law school."

"Oh, well, that sounds reasonable," Zoey said. "Nothing to flip your mom out."

Adam laughed. "Well, I think she was going to lose her mind if she saw me vegging out in front of the TV one more time," he said. "So it's just as well that I can come here and 'get some focus' in my life. And what about you, Zoey? What do you want to be when you grow up?"

Zoey sighed. "I've always wanted to be a writer," she said.

Adam studied her face. "Why do you sound so sad?"

"Oh, I just—" Zoey hesitated, and then decided to tell him the truth. "I saw this sign at the Historical Society," she said, and described the advertisement.

"Well, why don't you apply?" Adam asked.

Zoey rolled her eyes. "They didn't mean me!" she said.

"Why not? You're local, you're a writer."

"I think they want a local *published* writer," Zoey said. "It's a small difference, I realize, but I think they might feel strongly about it."

"But then again, they might not," Adam said. "You can at least apply, right?"

Zoey glanced at him and smiled. "I guess I could."

"Promise?" Adam said.

Zoey laughed. "If it's that important to you, sure, I promise."

"It's that important to me," Adam said.

He smiled at Zoey, and suddenly she felt as though it didn't matter that her clothes were grubby or her hair unwashed and her face shiny. For the first time in a long time, Zoey felt beautiful.

Three

Christopher swung his arms in a circle as he walked toward the back room and the overworked muscles in his shoulders gave off loud popping sounds, but he didn't even hear. He was too happy.

Mr. Passmore had said that he, Benjamin, Zoey, and Adam could certainly manage the restaurant over the weekend, which meant that Christopher could go visit Aisha. He couldn't wait to tell her.

Christopher hurried into the back room and dialed Aisha's number from memory.

"Hello?"

"Eesh?"

"No, it's Felicia. Is this Christopher?"

"It sure is. How are you, Felicia?"

"Oh, fine."

Christopher tried not to sound impatient. "Is Aisha there?"

"No," Felicia said. "She's out."

Christopher was mildly surprised. Aisha was usually home studying this time of night.

"Do you know when she'll be back?" he asked.

Felicia sounded thoughtful. "I'm not sure. She's out with whatshisname. . . ."

Christopher felt a flicker of unease. *Yes, by all means, what* is *his name?*

"Graham?" Felicia said. "Does that sound familiar?"

Christopher clenched his teeth. "No, actually, it doesn't."

"Well, she said he was an old friend," Felicia said. "Did you need to talk to her? Was it something important?"

Christopher sighed. "I just wanted to tell her that I could come visit this weekend."

"Oh, that's great," Felicia said. "I'm sure she'll be happy. When are you coming down?"

"I thought Saturday morning," Christopher said.

"Well, then, maybe I'll disappear on Saturday night," Felicia said. "Listen, Christopher, are you busy right now? Do you have time to take this questionnaire I'm supposed to give people for my psychology class?"

"Well . . ." Christopher hesitated.

"Please?" Felicia asked. "It's only about ten questions."

Christopher shrugged to himself. "Okay."

"All right," Felicia said, and he could hear a slight rustling of paper. "Here's your first question: What is the foremost erogenous zone? Feet, sexual organs, or mind?"

Christopher swallowed. "What kind of questionnaire is this?"

Felicia laughed. "It's for the human sexuality part of my psych class. It's supposed to reveal how little everyone actually knows about sex."

Well, if you'd told me that, I wouldn't have agreed to take it, Christopher thought. But he didn't want to sound cowardly or ignorant or whatever, so he just said, "I see. Well, uh, mind. I'd answer mind."

"Okay," Felicia said. "*Lingam* is another word for an aphrodisiac, a deep kiss, or a penis."

Christopher was silent for a full second. He couldn't believe she'd actually said that . . . word so coolly. He cleared his throat. "A kiss," he said, having no idea.

Felicia didn't seem fazed. "Okay. Which one of these herbs is considered an aphrodisiac? Garlic, ginseng, or oregano?"

"Oregano," Christopher said because he liked Italian food.

"Oh, that's right, you're a spaghetti man," Felicia said, as though she could read his mind. "Next question. A somnophiliac is someone who becomes aroused while *(a)* going without sleep, *(b)* sleepwalking, or *(c)* fondling a sleeping stranger."

"Um, *c*, I guess," Christopher said.

"In what work of literature does the longest sex scene appear?" Felicia asked. "*Ulysses, Lady Chatterly's Lover,* or *A Tale of Two Cities?*"

"*Lady Chatterly's Lover,*" Christopher guessed. He'd read the other two, and he couldn't remember any sex scenes in either one, long, short, or otherwise.

"Okay. And what percentage of junior high boys are responsible for junior-high-age pregnancies: 25 percent, 50 percent, or 75 percent?"

Christopher glanced at the open door to the restaurant. "Uh, 75 percent."

"Isn't that a disturbing question?" Felicia asked. "Don't you wish that *one hundred percent* was, like, at least one of the options?"

"Well, yeah, now that you mention it," Christopher said.

"Okay," Felicia said. "Do you prefer blonds or brunettes?"

"Blonds."

Felicia laughed. "That was a joke, Christopher."

"Oh." Christopher felt himself blushing. How stupid could he be? And why did he choose blonds?

"Well, listen, thanks a million," Felicia said. "I really appreciate it, long-distance and everything."

"It was no problem," Christopher said.

"So, what message should I give Aisha?" Felicia asked. "Do you want her to call you?"

Christopher hesitated. "No message," he said finally. "I'll call her back when I can."

"All right," Felicia said cheerfully. "Take care. And listen, I really had a good time last weekend."

"Me too," Christopher said. "Good-bye."

"Bye, Christopher."

He hung up, feeling a little bit sick to his stomach. He could only imagine what Aisha would say if she knew Felicia had given him that stupid sex quiz. But it wasn't his fault. She'd tricked him into it. Besides, it hadn't been very sexy, not really. Why, he'd had sexier conversations with Nina and Zoey, and Aisha had never cared.

So why didn't you leave a message? a voice spoke up in his mind.

Because there was no sense in having Aisha *know* he'd called and spoken to Felicia.

"Okay, Benjamin," Dr. Avery said, holding up the newspaper. "You know the routine."

Benjamin sighed. He had recently seen Dr. Martin in Boston, who told him that his recent vision problems didn't necessarily mean that his eyesight was failing. Still, he had referred Benjamin to Dr. Avery and recommended regular examinations, as it would be too much of a strain for Benjamin to travel to Boston all the time. So Benjamin had come to Dr. Avery, who had discovered among other things that Benjamin had memorized the eye chart. Now Dr. Avery tested his eyesight by making him read headlines.

"Tractor Digs Up Fresh Asphalt," he read dutifully.

"Okay," Dr. Avery said, turning the page and shaking out the newspaper. "Now this one."

"Church Supper Huge Success," Benjamin said. "What paper *is* this?"

"The *Murkville Gazette*," Dr. Avery said, grinning. "Population 149. Next headline, please."

Benjamin squinted. "Maude Has Rummage Sale."

Dr. Avery stopped smiling. "You're guessing," he said abruptly. "It's Mabel Has Garage Sale."

He tossed the paper aside and came over to shine his light in Benjamin's eyes. He sighed and sat down in his swivel chair, tapping the light thoughtfully against his palm.

"Bad news?" Benjamin asked.

Dr. Avery shrugged. "You're straining your eyes," he said. "And it's causing your vision to deteriorate."

Benjamin's hands tightened on the arms of the examination chair. "Is there anything you can do?"

"No, but there's something *you* can do," Dr. Avery said. "You're going to have to rest your eyes."

"Rest?" Benjamin said, relieved. "Will that fix it?"

Dr. Avery's face was serious. "I don't know, Benjamin," he said. "No one knows exactly why you went blind in the first place because most people with acute-angle glaucoma retain at least partial vision. And the surgery that restored your sight was experimental and not successful in all cases, so no one really knows why you can see now."

Benjamin sighed.

"I know that's not the answer you were hoping for," Dr. Avery said. "But all I can do is prescribe complete eye rest for a minimum of four hours per day. Lie in a darkened room and use an eye mask."

"Four hours?" Benjamin said. "That's nothing. I usually sleep eight, anyway."

"This is in addition to your sleep," Dr. Avery said.

"In addition!" Benjamin said. "Four hours! What will I tell people?"

Dr. Avery looked at him, and his face was kind. "The truth?" he suggested.

Four

"*Both* hands on the wheel, Nina!" Burke Geiger shouted.

"Dad, we're not even *moving* yet," Nina said, unperturbed. She shook a Lucky Strike out of the pack and put it between her lips, unlit. "Will you please chill out?"

"How can I chill down when you were just in a fender bender two days ago?" Burke asked.

"Dad, that accident was one hundred percent not my fault," Nina said, putting the car in gear and driving down the Geigers' circular driveway. "Besides, it's chill *out,* not chill *down.* I wish you wouldn't use slang you don't understand."

"He's just trying to relate to you, dear," Nina's stepmother, Sarah, said from the backseat.

"Well, he can relate to me in normal, everyday English," Nina said. "I'm not some juvenile delinquent in a movie of the week. He doesn't have to come down to my *level.*"

"What does the movie of the week have to do with anything?" Burke asked. "And getting back to the accident not being your fault, the police said you were tailgating."

"Yes, but who stopped for absolutely no reason?"

Nina asked. "The guy in front of me! Everything would have been fine if he hadn't slammed on his brakes out of the blue."

"He was turning into his own driveway," Sarah said.

"Well, all the more reason he should have slowed down beforehand," Nina said.

"Do you know how much my insurance premiums went up because of that accident?" Burke said. "Nina, you're drifting into that lane."

"I am *not*," Nina lied, pulling back into her own lane. "Sarah, will you please keep him on a leash? He's driving me crazy. Now, where do you guys want to go for dinner?"

"Oh, how about Bœuf à la Mode?" Burke suggested.

"Beef with ice cream?" Nina asked. "What kind of a name is that?"

"Nina—"

"Besides, I don't want to go anywhere fancy."

"But you said we couldn't go to Houlihan's or Applebee's because someone from school might see you," Sarah protested.

"Yes, and that's still true," Nina said. "You have to understand that my social status is, like, one millimeter above Julius McMartin's, and being seen eating dinner with my parents might drop me even lower."

"Who is Julius McMartin?" Burke asked.

"He's this calculus nerd who never does anything but study for his SATs and think of things to put on his college applications."

"It wouldn't hurt you to study more for your SATs," Burke said.

"I do study," Nina protested, speeding up to make

33

the light. "I memorized all those stupid vocabulary flash cards."

"Nina, we just took that corner on two wheels!" Burke shouted.

"We did not," Nina said. "Stop exaggerating. Two wheels! What hyperbowl."

Burke frowned. "What what?"

"Hyperbowl. It's an SAT vocab word."

"Hyperbole," Burke said, enunciating loudly. "Not hyperbowl, for heaven's sake."

"Well, it's a *written* test," Nina said. "I know how to spell it."

"Nina—," Sarah said, "that car in front of us—"

"That's hardly the point," Burke said, ignoring Sarah. "Like earlier when you thought *bœuf à la mode* meant beef with ice cream—"

"Nina—," Sarah said.

"Well, what does it mean?" Nina demanded. "Just what does it mean, then?"

"Nina!" Sarah shouted.

But the only sound that answered her was the sickening crunch of metal as Nina rear-ended the car in front of them.

"Clara, Clara," Paolo said as he lounged at the bed by her open suitcase. "Won't you please come home with me for the weekend?"

"No," Claire said, folding a silk blouse and putting it into the suitcase.

"Come on," Paolo coaxed. "It'll be romantic. Much like this wonderful picture of you in the seventh grade with a perm."

"Paolo, I really can't think of anything less romantic than meeting your parents," Claire said.

"And I'm not going to let you look at my photo album if you keep making fun of it."

"I can't help it," Paolo said. "It's just so hilarious." He turned the album so she could see the page he was looking at. "Does your sister ever open her eyes?"

"Of course she does," Claire said irritably. "She just doesn't like the flash, and she always blinks ahead of time." She pulled four pairs of tights and a camisole out of a drawer and tucked them into the suitcase.

"Excuse me, but how long are you going for?" Paolo asked. "A month?"

"Excuse *me*," Claire said, "but what business is it of yours?"

Paolo was unperturbed. "Do you ever wish you were a boy and packing just meant throwing a pair of boxer shorts into a paper bag?"

"No, Paolo," Claire said. "I can honestly say I've never wished I were a boy."

Paolo grinned. "Well, then, we have something in common because I have never wished you were a boy, either." He closed the photo album and turned on his side, resting his head on his hand. "Are you sure you don't want to come home with me?"

"Very sure."

"You could hear how my dad makes us sing 'Greensleeves' in rounds before dinner."

"Paolo," Claire said, shaking out a T-shirt. "You know how a minute ago I said I was very sure? Well, that little tidbit made me *twice* as sure."

"But why?"

"Isn't singing in rounds reason enough?" Claire asked. She tried to shut her suitcase and failed.

"Well, don't you want to see the room where I grew up and picture me as a little boy?" Paolo asked.

Claire looked at his sparkling dark eyes, full of mischief. She smiled wryly. "Believe it or not, I don't need to see your bedroom to picture you as a little boy."

Paolo sighed and opened the album again.

Claire pushed down on the top of the suitcase and snapped the latch closed with difficulty.

Paolo was snickering.

"What now?" she asked.

He pointed to a picture. "Your stepmother. Why is she wearing that helmet?"

"That's not a helmet, that's her hair," Claire said. She jerked the album away from him. "How would you like it if I came over to your house and mocked all your relatives?"

"I'm *begging* you to come to my house and mock all my relatives," Paolo protested. He slid abruptly to the floor and clutched at her skirt. "Please, Claire? Please, please, please?"

Claire sighed. She touched his hair and shook her head. "Okay," she said. "I give up. I'll come home with you."

Aisha

Today I read <u>Cosmo</u> when I should have been studying, and there was this big article called "Roommate Horror Stories," and of course I couldn't resist reading it.

Actually, at first it made me feel better because these were really horrifying horror stories. One girl's roommate pawned her watch, and another girl thought she had lost a ring belonging to her grandmother, until she saw it on her former roommate's finger three years later. One guy came home to find every stick of furniture gone and an eviction notice in the mail. One girl's roommate even used the girl's social security number to apply for credit cards!

I was sitting there feeling better and better, thinking, "Boy, I can live with Felicia borrowing my clothes all the time," and then I read the last story.

It was about this girl who came home one afternoon to find her "blond bombshell" of a roommate in bed with her fiancé. Sound like anyone we know?

Five

"Adam!" Zoey shouted, throwing open the swinging doors to the kitchen.

"Ouch!" a voice cried. "What?"

"Oh, my God, I'm so sorry," Zoey said, hurrying through the doors to where Adam stood rubbing his shoulder. "Those doors are lethal. I did exactly the same thing to Benjamin a week ago. We should get them removed."

Adam smiled painfully. "Or you could stop catapulting through them."

"Oh, I know, but I was so excited," Zoey said, smiling up at him. "I have the best news! Sit down and let me fix you an ice pack for your shoulder."

"I don't need an ice pack, Zoey," Adam said, sitting down. "What's your news?"

"You do so need an ice pack," Zoey said, going to the large freezer in the corner. "Benjamin had the worst goose egg. . . ." She knelt down and took several ice cubes out of the freezer. "Anyway, my news is that I called the Historical Society this morning and they gave me the job."

Adam grinned. "That's terrific." He winced. "I'll hug you when I can move my arm again."

Zoey moved behind him and pressed the towel-wrapped ice against his shoulder. "I really am awfully sorry."

"Don't worry, I'm just teasing you," Adam said. "How did you get the job?"

"I lied," Zoey said, smiling. "I told the woman that I worked at the Smithsonian in Washington and that I had all this historical interest and stuff."

"Is any of that true?" Adam asked.

Zoey considered. "Well, I did live in Washington for two weeks, and I walked past the Smithsonian every day."

"Well, then, that's barely lying," Adam said, his eyes twinkling.

"Oh, stop it, it was your idea in the first place," Zoey said. She removed the ice pack. "How's your shoulder?"

"Numb."

"Good." She put the ice pack back in place. Even sitting down, Adam's head was almost level with her shoulders, and Zoey could smell the clean scent of his hair. She thought idly that boys always smelled so much more interesting than girls. Girls smelled like Obsession or Red Door, but boys all had their own smells, different combinations of shampoo and toothpaste and sweat and soap. Lucas smelled like—

Zoey forced her mind away from Lucas, but her eyes strayed to the kitchen window. She could see Lucas working on the bare frame of her new house. He was there almost all the time now that fishing was off-season. Her father went up there constantly to talk to him, and Zoey could barely control her temper when Mr. Passmore told her, "Lucas says the house is coming along," or "Lucas thinks the dining

40

room should be a brick and a half wider," or "Lucas is worth his weight in gold."

"Zoey?" It was Adam, and she could tell from the way he sounded that it wasn't the first time he'd said her name.

"Hmmm?"

"Who is that guy?" he asked, gesturing toward the window.

Zoey pressed the ice pack more firmly against Adam's shoulder. "His name is Lucas Cabral."

"Yes, but *who* is he?" Adam asked. "Who is he to *you?*"

"He's no one to me," Zoey said stiffly. "He's just my ex-boyfriend."

"Oh," Adam said. "That explains it."

Zoey frowned. "Explains what?"

"Why every time you catch sight of him, you look like someone's out there kicking your dog," Adam said. "How long ago did you break up?"

"About a month," Zoey said.

"Well, it takes a while to get over people sometimes," Adam said. He hesitated. "Especially if they've hurt you."

Zoey lifted her chin. "I am completely over Lucas," she said coolly. "I'm grateful to him for working on the house, and that's it."

"Oh, really?" Adam caught her free hand in his. "You're really over him?"

His eyes were searching hers for something. She didn't know what. "Yes," she said. "Really."

Adam released her hand. "Well, then, you should be nicer to him. He came in here yesterday to talk to Benjamin, and you left the room."

"So?" Zoey asked. The ice was starting to leave a damp patch on Adam's shirt, so she threw the cubes in the sink. "I may be over Lucas, but that doesn't mean I want to be around him."

Adam stretched and stood up. "Well, I guess you know best about that," he said. "But he would probably get the message if you could just treat him the same way you treat everyone else."

Suddenly he wrapped his arms around her shoulders from behind. "There's your hug," he said, releasing her. "Congratulations. Now I have to get back to work. See you later."

"See you," Zoey said faintly. Her eyes were still on Lucas.

Lucas was so busy measuring the space for the Passmores' window that he could almost forget the question that been bothering him for the last twenty hours:

Who was that guy?

The big, broad-shouldered one. The one Zoey had been walking next to yesterday. She had been listening to him so intently that she was frowning and nodding at the same time. What had they been talking about? And who *was* he?

And why wasn't anyone talking about it? One of the things that Lucas hated about Chatham Island was how everyone knew what everyone else was doing, or thought they knew, and talked about nothing else day and night. And now, when he finally wanted to know something, no one was talking. Lucas had kept his ears open at the marina, at home, at the store, at the construction site, but nobody had said, "Hey, did you see Zoey Passmore with—"

With who?

Lucas shook his head and began measuring the

window space again. He didn't want the Passmores' window to be off center just because he was having paranoid thoughts. Not that he *was*. He was just curious.

"Lucas?"

He turned around. It was Zoey, standing there with an aluminum pan in her hands. Steam was escaping from under the pan's cover.

Zoey opened her mouth and shut it several times, as though she were rejecting sentences before she even started them. Finally she just held the pan out in front of her and said, "I thought you might be hungry."

"Thank you," Lucas said uncertainly. He was in fact hungry. He was always hungry. He took the pie pan.

Zoey hesitated. "It's just a fried-egg sandwich," she said. Then quickly, "My dad made it."

Did she say that so I wouldn't think she *made it?* Lucas wondered.

"I love fried-egg sandwiches," Lucas said. He pried the cardboard cover off and then looked up. "Keep me company?"

Zoey bit her lip. "Sure."

Lucas sat on a pile of lumber and took a bite of his sandwich. Zoey sat gingerly on a pile of lumber opposite him.

"So," she said, "am I sitting in the kitchen or what?"

Lucas smiled faintly. "The laundry room."

Zoey frowned. "We don't have a laundry room."

"You do now," Lucas said, taking another bite of his sandwich. "Your mom wants one."

"She does?" Zoey said, puzzled. "How do you know?"

"She told me," Lucas said simply. "I went to see her."

Zoey looked surprised. "You went to see my mom in the hospital?"

"Sure." Lucas finished the last bite of the sandwich. "Just because she's in the hospital doesn't mean she shouldn't have a say in her own house."

"But the way she—looks," Zoey said awkwardly.

"She looked okay to me," Lucas said. He met Zoey's eyes. "Really. She looked fine. A little tired and pale, but fine."

Zoey smiled at him, the first real smile he'd seen from her since they broke up. "Oh, good," she said softly.

Lucas smiled back. "Thanks for the sandwich," he said gently.

"Oh, you're welcome," she said absently. "Well, I'd better get back to work."

She rose, and he got to his feet reluctantly. "It looks like you have help at the restaurant," he said casually.

Zoey seemed confused, and then she said, "Oh, Adam? He's my cousin. He's going to help us out for a while."

Cousin? Lucas thought. *That's too good to be true.*

"Thanks again," he said. "For the sandwich and the company."

"I—I could bring you something else sometime, maybe," Zoey said cautiously.

"That would be great," Lucas said, not wanting to push. But his spirits were soaring. What had come over Zoey? Why was she acting this way? Was she—forgiving him? "If you want to, that would be great. I really appreciate it."

44

Zoey gave him an odd, lopsided smile. "Well, Adam suggested it," she said. "He says that I can't go on hating you forever, that I have to treat you like everyone else." She gave him a small wave. "See you later," she said, and started back down the hill.

And if she noticed that Lucas looked as though someone had just turned out the sun, she didn't show it.

BENJAMIN

Last night Kalif asked me if blind
people can see in their dreams,
which is a pretty interesting question. Because they don't. Actually
they do at first. I remember that
from when I was twelve, right after I
went blind, and how I loved to go to
sleep and have glorious Technicolor
dreams all night long. But then after
a few months the dreams grew less
frequent and less colorful until
finally they just stopped altogether,
and for the next seven years my
dreams were strictly auditory.

Since Kalif reminded me of that,
I've decided to use my "resting" time
to try to commit various images to
memory so that if . . . the unthink-
able happens, I can be better prepared.

This is what I want to remember:

My father's face when he's tasting
the spaghetti sauce.

How my mother looked once when
we met unexpectedly on the street
and her face lit up.

The way Zoey looks when you tease her and she knows she shouldn't rise to the bait, but she does, anyway.

How the island looks when you're approaching on the ferry and everything is so beautiful that even the rusted metal on the landing is the most glorious shade of red.

Oriental rugs, which always felt just like any other carpets but actually contain every color in the world.

The difference between gold and yellow.

Whitecaps.

Nina when she's smiling.

Nina when she's concentrating.

Nina.

Six

Aisha was just coming back from aerobics when she met Felicia in the hallway, returning from breakfast in the cafeteria. Aisha knew she looked all red faced and sweaty, and here was Felicia, looking beautiful and composed in flannel pants and a green turtleneck sweater.

"Hi," Aisha said, wondering why they never seemed to meet when she, Aisha, was all dressed up and *Felicia* was coming back from aerobics. But then Aisha supposed it still wouldn't matter because Felicia would *still* manage to look gorgeous and Aisha would *still* feel like someone's dowdy little sister.

I should really stop comparing myself to her, Aisha thought, *because I never, ever win.* It was a depressing thought.

"Are you okay?" Felicia asked.

"Oh, yeah, fine," Aisha answered.

"Because you looked a little funny there for a second," Felicia said.

They walked down the hall toward their room together.

"You look nice," Aisha said.

"Thanks," Felicia said. "I'm going out to lunch after class."

Aisha wondered who Felicia was having lunch with. It occurred to her that she knew next to nothing about Felicia's personal life.

Felicia unlocked the door, and they walked in. Aisha threw her gym bag on her bed.

"Hey, we have a message," Felicia said happily, pressing the play button on the answering machine.

Aisha wondered why Felicia was so excited—she got messages all the time.

The answering machine clicked, and Aisha stripped off her damp T-shirt as she listened. She smiled. It was Christopher.

"Hi, Eesh, it's me. I can get this weekend off, and I thought I'd come visit you again if you don't have a horrible test or something. Give me a call. Bye."

"That's great about this weekend," Felicia said, rewinding the tape. "I thought so when Christopher called last night."

Aisha's smile faded. "Christopher called last night?"

"Uh-huh. You were out with Graham." Felicia dug through the pile of cosmetics on her dresser. "Damn. Where's my red lipstick?"

"Why didn't you tell me he called?" Aisha persisted. Her skin was starting to goose bump around the edges of her sports bra.

"He didn't leave a message," Felicia said casually. "Oh, here it is," she added triumphantly, holding up a lipstick. She turned toward the mirror and began applying it.

Aisha felt as though things were moving in slow motion. "And Christopher told you that he was coming up here this weekend?"

"Uh-huh," Felicia said, parting her lips slightly and applying another coat of lipstick.

Aisha swallowed. There was absolutely no reason that Christopher had to tell Aisha that he was coming up for the weekend before he told anyone else.

No *rational* reason.

"By the way," Felicia added. She was putting on yet *another* coat of lipstick, Aisha noticed. "Christopher and I talked about it, and we decided that you could probably use some time alone with him, so if he does come, just let me know and I'll disappear."

Aisha's heart was suddenly beating more rapidly than it had during her entire aerobics class. She sank slowly down onto her bed.

Felicia and Christopher had *decided?* They had *talked about it* and *the two of them* thought Aisha needed time alone with Christopher? Had she heard right? Christopher had discussed her with Felicia? Their relationship? Aisha? Aisha's *needs?*

She didn't even notice that Felicia was watching her in the mirror.

"I mean it," Felicia continued, as though Aisha had spoken. "It's no problem whatsoever." She glanced at her watch. "Oh, shoot, I'm running late."

She gathered up her books.

Aisha stayed where she was on her bed, her heart slamming against her rib cage in such a violent way that she thought she might throw up.

Felicia didn't seem to notice. "Just leave me a note or whatever after you speak to Christopher," she said lightly. She squeezed Aisha's shoulder, and then she was gone.

Aisha stared after her. *What did she want me to do?* she wondered. *Thank her?*

* * *

Nina arrived at her first driving lesson wearing a moth-eaten red velvet coatdress over leggings and carrying her favorite striped cotton bag with the long fringe.

She walked across the parking lot to where a bald man was leaning against a car. On top of the car was a sign that read Champion Traffic School.

"Hello," Nina said, sticking out her hand. "You must be Mr. Samuels."

"I am," Mr. Samuels said laconically, taking her hand. He didn't stand up straight. "And you?"

"Nina Geiger, your student," Nina said, rummaging around in her purse. She produced a small white bakery bag and held it in one hand while she kept searching with the other.

Mr. Samuels looked interested. "Are those doughnuts?"

"Hmmm?" Nina said absently. "Oh, yeah." She handed him the bag. "Help yourself, but leave the apple fritter." She pulled a miniature carton of milk out of her purse and set it on the hood of the car. Then she produced a straw and jammed it into the milk.

Finally she found what she was looking for. She retrieved a pack of Lucky Strikes and shook one out. "Listen," she said, placing the unlit cigarette between her lips. "I just want to tell you that I'm only here to reduce my dad's insurance premiums. There is *nothing* wrong with my driving."

Mr. Samuels had just taken a big bite of doughnut, and he chewed it while he looked at her. Then he swallowed and picked a manila folder off the roof of the car. Without a word he opened it.

"What is that?" Nina asked. "My chart? I'm not a hospital patient."

"It's your insurance record." Mr. Samuels took a pair of half-moon glasses out of his shirt pocket and put them on. He began reading:

December 15: Rear-end collision with a lawfully parked vehicle. Damage, $400. Policyholder at fault.

February 18: Out-of-lane collision. Damage, $1,200. Policyholder at fault.

March 17: Failure to proceed with due caution from a traffic signal resulting in rear-end collision. Damage, $100. Policyholder at fault.

June 27: Collision while making illegal U-turn across the travel path of a vehicle traveling in the same direction. Damage, $1,500. Policyholder at fault.

October 12: Failure to obey speed limit resulting in rear-end collision. Damage, $750. Policyholder at fault.

Nina was silent.

"Do you have anything to add?" Mr. Samuels asked.

"Yes," Nina said. "I am really, really happy that I didn't let you eat my apple fritter. Now, let's get in the car and get this over with."

"We have to wait for the other pupil," Mr. Samuels said.

"Other pupil?" Nina repeated. "I thought these were private driving lessons."

"Semiprivate," Mr. Samuels said shortly. "Here she is."

Nina heard footsteps behind her and turned.

In a second she took in the dark blond hair, the willowy body, the startled blue eyes. It was Zoey.

Zoey gasped, and Nina turned immediately back to Mr. Samuels.

She and Zoey spoke at exactly the same moment and with the same inflection. It couldn't have been more simultaneous if it had been digitally recorded.

"No way," they both said.

Seven

Paolo seemed happy as he drove Claire's car through Kingston, the tiny suburb of Princeton where he grew up. Claire tried to seem happy, too, although she was incredibly nervous.

"There's where I went to high school," he said, pointing. "That's the McDonald's parking lot where everyone used to go to make out."

"A McDonald's?" Claire said, trying to appear as though she were paying attention. "That doesn't sound very romantic."

Paolo considered. "Maybe not, but it's the only place where you could go that the cops wouldn't find you."

"Why did the cops care?" Claire asked, surprised.

"Excellent question," Paolo said. "Personally, I think the parents must have paid them because the cops always knew every kid by name, and they would shine their flashlights in your face and say, *Paolo, Paolo, what will your mother say?*"

Claire laughed. "I suppose you got caught all the time," she said, amused.

"Oh, not really," Paolo said. "I wasn't that interested in girls in high school."

"Paolo, high school was *two months* ago," Claire

pointed out. "And you're certainly interested in girls now."

"Hey, that's true," he said, surprised. "Maybe it was something about the girls in high school. They were always slipping notes into my locker that had, like, little tiny hearts instead of punctuation."

Claire rolled her eyes. Why did he have to be so weird when she was feeling so nervous and queasy? Every time they turned a corner, she was afraid Paolo would say, *Here we are,* and then it would be time to face the family.

She flipped down the sun visor and examined her reflection in the mirror. Her heart rose a little. She was wearing a severely tailored gray suit that she felt made her look older and more professional. She'd pulled her hair back into a knot and was wearing lots of eyeliner. She looked composed and elegant, even if that wasn't how she felt.

"Here we are," Paolo said, slowing the car and turning into a long circular drive that led to a large brick house with white pillars.

Claire looked at the house and then back at Paolo. "Didn't you tell me your dad was in construction?" she asked.

He grinned. "He is in construction—he owns a bunch of construction companies."

Claire sighed and looked back at the imposing house. For the first time she felt a pang of sympathy for the boys in high school who'd had to schlepp up the walk to her big brick house.

Paolo parked the car, and they went up to the front porch. Paolo opened the door, and Claire followed him into a large foyer.

"Hello?" Paolo called. "Anyone home?"

Immediately answering calls and footsteps came

from every direction as Paolo's family rushed to greet him. His mother came hurrying in first. She was short and pretty, with a dark elfin haircut.

While she hugged Paolo, Claire saw his sisters coming down the stairs. Paolo had already told her their names and ages: Marta, twenty; Isabel, sixteen; and Elena, fifteen. They were all wearing jeans and sweaters, and they all had thick, dark hair that hung below their shoulders.

Claire felt her panic rising. *They're so pretty!* she thought in a moment of threatened vanity. *But my hair is shinier than any of theirs. Why didn't I wear it loose? Oh, why did I wear this stupid suit? I look like a jerk.*

And yet when they shook hands with her, she saw only curiosity in their eyes and not competition. Claire had never known any girls who didn't view her as a rival—except for Nina.

And then Mr. O'Connell showed up, a handsome older man with a freckled face. He hugged Paolo and shook hands with Claire while the youngest sister, Elena, said, "Paolo, you missed all the excitement this morning. Dad practically got arrested for shoplifting!"

Mr. O'Connell made a wry face. "I was at the Home Depot, and when I went to pay the cashier, I pulled my money out of my pocket and she saw all these screws and bolts and stuff—"

"Dad carries a bunch of hardware in his pockets at all times," Marta explained to Claire.

"—and the cashier got all suspicious and called security, and they questioned me for about fifteen minutes," Paolo's dad finished as the O'Connells cracked up. Claire tried to laugh, too, but her lips felt cold, and she could barely smile.

Paolo's mother smiled at her. "Claire, are you tired?" she asked. "Should I show you to your room?"

Claire swallowed. "Yes, thank you," she said softly.

"I thought I would put you in the guest room," Paolo's mother continued. "And Paolo can sleep in his room."

"Okay, Ma," Paolo said. "Our rooms have been identified. Don't worry, we weren't planning to sleep together in grandma's four-poster bed."

Shut up, Paolo! Claire thought fiercely.

"Oh, shut up, Paolo," Mrs. O'Connell said good-naturedly. "Come with me, Claire."

Claire followed her up the curving staircase. Mrs. O'Connell kept up a steady stream of chatter, for which Claire was grateful.

Mrs. O'Connell opened a bedroom door. "This is our guest room," she said. She smiled tentatively. "Paolo's room is just down the hall. I'm not as old-fashioned as he thinks."

Claire returned the smile and looked around the guest room. "This is so beautiful," she said softly. She was afraid she sounded insincere, but she meant it. The room was large and sunny, done in shades of blue and green with lavender accents. "Oh, Mrs. O'Connell," she said. "I meant to give you this earlier."

Claire opened her purse and pulled out the bag of gourmet coffee beans she had brought as a hostess gift. "Paolo told me that you drink coffee," she said. "I love this brand, and I thought you might enjoy it."

"Thank you, Claire," Mrs. O'Connell said. She looked strained suddenly, and Claire wondered what had happened.

Then a flash of color on the floor caught her eye. It was the condom Paolo had accepted on campus and stuffed into her purse. It must have fallen out when she reached in for the coffee.

Claire felt the blood drain from her face.

"Come down whenever you're ready, Claire," Paolo's mother said quickly, and left the room.

Claire turned and threw her suitcase savagely on the bed, two bright spots of color flaming on her cheeks.

She wanted to swear, but she didn't know any words bad enough.

Nina! Zoey thought, horrified. *What's she doing here? Well, I don't care what she's doing here—I won't take driving lessons with her.*

"I won't take driving lessons with her," she said out loud to the bald man who she assumed was the teacher.

"I won't take driving lessons with *her*," Nina said.

The bald man finished his doughnut and brushed the crumbs from his hands. "Ladies, does this look like kindergarten?" he asked. "Because it's not. Now, I'm sorry you two haven't learned to share, but I don't cater to the whims of teenagers."

He picked up a manila folder from the roof of the car and flipped it open. "Ms. Passmore?" he asked.

Zoey didn't like the way he emphasized the *Ms.*, like he was humoring her feminist whims or something.

"Yes," she said sullenly.

"I'm Mr. Samuels," the bald man said. He scanned whatever was in the folder. "I see you have a lead foot."

Over his shoulder Nina looked so triumphant that Zoey wanted to slap her.

"One ticket," she said. "I got *one* ticket."

Mr. Samuels closed the folder. "All right, let's get started," he said. "First I'm just going to observe your driving abilities or lack thereof." He held out a set of keys to Zoey. "Ms. Passmore, please drive us in the general direction of Baltimore Avenue. Any route will do."

Zoey's brows drew together. "How come I have to go first?"

"As I said, this isn't kindergarten." Mr. Samuels sighed. When she didn't show any signs of moving, he added, "Because I said so."

Zoey took the keys and marched around to the driver's side. Mr. Samuels got in the passenger seat, and Nina climbed in back.

Zoey started the engine.

"We'd better fasten our seat belts," Nina said cheerfully to Mr. Samuels.

"Shut up," Zoey snapped, furious. She stomped on the accelerator, and the car leaped forward with a squeal of tires.

"Whoa!" Mr. Samuels said.

I'm not a horse, Zoey thought. *Jerk.*

"What a good thing no one in *this* car has a problem with speeding," Nina said from the back.

"Will you be quiet?" Zoey demanded, glancing over her shoulder. "I may be—fast, but at least I can drive. Did you know," she said, turning to Mr. Samuels, "that the first time *she* ever backed a car out of a garage, she took a foot off the edge of the garage door?"

"I repaired that," Nina said indignantly. "I even repainted. My dad never found out."

"So what does that mean?" Zoey asked. "That it didn't happen?"

"Well, did you know," Nina said, leaning forward to tap Mr. Samuels on the shoulder, "that when *she* took driver's ed the first time and they went downtown to do the parallel-parking test, she went back and forth so many times that a man ran out of the barbershop with shaving cream on his face to move his car?"

"He was paranoid," Zoey said. "I was doing fine. Did you know that Nina once—"

"How would I know any of these things?" Mr. Samuels interrupted. "I'm tired of you two bouncing your insults off me. If you have something to say, say it to each other."

"We have *nothing* to say to each other," Zoey said immediately.

"Yeah," Nina echoed.

"Well, good," Mr. Samuels said. "Maybe we can have some peace and quiet, then."

They drove along in silence for about ninety seconds.

"You could take your turns a little wider," Mr. Samuels said mildly.

"I'll say," Nina chimed in.

"It was a perfectly acceptable turn," Zoey protested.

"Tell that to whoever owned that poor mailbox," Nina muttered.

Zoey glared at her in the rearview mirror. "I did not hit a mailbox!"

"*Nicked* is probably a better word," Nina agreed.

"Girls," Mr. Samuels said warningly, and they fell quiet. Mr. Samuels made a note on his clipboard.

"Zoey, pull into that 7-Eleven and we'll switch drivers."

"No," Zoey said.

Mr. Samuels rolled his eyes. "What's the problem now?"

"I'm not pulling into a 7-Eleven parking lot," Zoey said, "because they are the most dangerous places on earth. Everyone is way too busy drinking a Slurpee to watch where they're going."

Zoey noticed Nina watching her in the mirror with a strange expression. Suddenly Zoey realized something. *Nina* was the one who had always said that about 7-Elevens. She had just parroted one of Nina's opinions word for word.

Zoey dropped her eyes.

"Fine," Mr. Samuels said. "Pull into the dry cleaners, then."

Zoey put on her turn signal, but she still felt confused and bewildered. Why would she be quoting someone she hated so much?

Eight

Christopher was trying to imagine why Aisha hadn't called him back yet. It wasn't like her. Maybe she had a class. Maybe she was studying for an exam. Maybe the phones were out in her dorm.

Or maybe she's with that Graham, his mind suggested helpfully.

He couldn't deny that it was possible she was with Graham. Maybe she'd been with Graham all night, although the rational part of Christopher's brain admitted that this was pretty unlikely since Christopher and Aisha were *engaged* and she'd never spent the night. Still, it made him wonder.

At two in the afternoon he broke down and called her from the back room of the restaurant. She answered on the first ring.

"Hello?"

"Aisha? It's me."

"Oh, hi," she said in a voice that was barely louder than a whisper.

"How are you?" Christopher asked cautiously.

"I'm . . . okay," she said, and sniffled.

Christopher knew from long experience that he was supposed to say, *You don't sound okay,* and then Aisha would say, *Of course I'm not!* and tell him what was wrong. He took a deep breath. "You don't sound okay."

"Of course I'm not okay!" Aisha practically wailed. "How *can* I be when I'm so hurt?"

"Hurt by what?" Christopher asked patiently.

"By that conversation you had with Felicia!" she cried.

Christopher closed his eyes. She had found out about the sex quiz. He should have known she would. Felicia must have told her, or maybe she found out some other way, and now he was somehow going to have to cast a better light on this and—

"Oh, Christopher," Aisha said. "How could you? How could you discuss our weekend with Felicia before you even told me?"

Christopher opened his eyes. "What?"

"You heard me," Aisha said. "Do you know how it makes me feel that you and *Felicia* decided that she should go away this weekend?"

Christopher said nothing; his mind was working rapidly. "You're angry about this weekend?" he asked finally, trying to find out exactly where he stood.

"Angry and hurt," Aisha clarified. "And betrayed and upset and—"

"By what, exactly?" Christopher interrupted before she could add any more adjectives.

"By the fact that you and Felicia discussed me and decided that I needed more time alone with you," Aisha said. "You and I are the ones who should make that decision, Christopher. Not you and her."

Christopher frowned, trying to remember if that's exactly how the conversation had gone. "It wasn't like that," he began, but he wasn't quite sure what it had been like. "Besides, Eesh, you were mad last weekend because she *was* around. And now you're mad because she *won't* be around?"

Aisha was silent for a moment. "No," she said finally. "I'm glad she's not going to be around. I just—I don't know. I wanted to be the one who decided she shouldn't be."

Christopher sighed. "Well, what do you want me to do now?"

Her answer was immediate. "I want you to listen to how angry I am with her."

Christopher smiled faintly. "I could do that this weekend," he said. "I could drive down, and you could tell me how angry you are for hours and hours."

"Oh, true," Aisha said, and he knew she was smiling, too. "But what will we do when I'm done telling you?"

"I'll think of something," Christopher assured her. "You leave that to me."

"Benjamin?" He heard his door open. "Oh, sorry, I didn't know you were sleeping."

Even before he pulled off his eye mask, Benjamin knew it was Nina. "It's okay," he said, squinting at her. "Come on in."

She walked into the room he shared with Kalif and sat on the other twin bed, looking around. "Wow, so this is where you live now, huh? What's it like to share a room with Kalif?"

Benjamin had been living in one of the Grays' guest rooms until Mr. Passmore came home and insisted that it was wrong to take up space in the B&B that should be reserved for paying customers. So Benjamin had been moved into Kalif's room.

"Close your eyes and imagine what it's like," Benjamin said.

"Okay . . . ," Nina said, and he was amused to see that she actually did have her eyes closed.

"Well, it's worse than that," he said.

She opened her eyes. "Really? Does he try to make you wet the bed or something?"

Benjamin frowned. "How do you make someone wet the bed?"

She shrugged. "Supposedly by soaking their wrists in hot water. At least that's what they told us at camp."

"Oh," he said, nodding. "Well, I did wake up with my hand in a bowl of water the other day." He saw her looking at him. "It didn't work," he added wryly.

"Oh, I always wondered," she said, sounding sincerely disappointed. "Well, listen, I just came over to see if you wanted to go to a movie with me."

"I can't," he said. "I have to rest."

"I see," Nina said, and her voice was cold.

Benjamin reached out and grabbed her arm. "No, really," he said, and paused. "My doctor prescribed eye rest, four hours of it a day. That's why I was wearing the eye mask."

Of all the possible responses, Nina's was the best and most immediate he could think of.

"Oh," she said. "Should I read to you?"

Benjamin's heart rose at the thought, but he hesitated. "You don't have to do that."

"I know," Nina said impatiently. "I'm *offering*."

"Well, I can't afford to pay you."

"That's okay," Nina said, walking over to the bookshelf. "Truthfully, I was never in it for the money, anyway."

*   *   *

Claire felt marginally better that night when she walked back toward the guest room after brushing her teeth. Earlier she had changed into a miniskirt and plain turtleneck sweater, washed off that dumb eyeliner, and worn her hair loose and bouncy to dinner.

Dinner had—thankfully!—gone okay, although Paolo's father did make them sing in rounds. Claire had only mouthed the song because she didn't want anyone to hear her singing off-key. Then after dinner the whole family had prepared trays and trays of hors d'oeuvres for a party the O'Connells were throwing the next day. Paolo and his sisters and his parents had talked and laughed and teased each other at top volume the whole time, and Claire was glad that at least no one expected her to make conversation. Afterward they all watched a movie together, which was also fine with Claire because no one expected her to talk then, either. Just why she was so tongue-tied around Paolo's family, she didn't know. But she was happy when the movie was over and everyone decided to go to bed.

As she passed Paolo's room on the way back from brushing her teeth Claire noticed the door was ajar and stopped. She knocked lightly on the door frame.

Paolo was lying on his bed, flipping through an elderly-looking issue of *Highlights*. "Hey," he said, looking up and smiling. "Come in."

Claire entered and shut the door behind her. "Why are you reading *Highlights*?"

He shrugged and smiled. "My mom never canceled my subscription," he said. He reached out and took her hand. "Now, tell me what's wrong."

Claire sat on the edge of his bed, and Paolo ran a

finger along the inside of her wrist. A shiver went up Claire's spine, and she casually disengaged her hand. "Nothing's wrong," she said.

"You've been quiet all evening."

"Well, what do you expect?" she asked. "I was so embarrassed; I couldn't even look your mom in the face."

Paolo looked surprised. "Why not?"

"Because *you*"—Claire said, poking him in the chest—"stuffed that stupid condom in my purse, and it fell out right in front of her."

Paolo laughed delightedly. "What did she do, cross herself?"

"It's not funny!" Claire protested.

"Oh, come on," Paolo said. "My mom's been through worse than that."

"Knowing you, I can believe it," Claire said wryly.

Paolo gently pulled her down on the bed next to him. She rested her head on his chest.

"So when is your conference tomorrow?" Paolo asked, stroking her hair.

"Um, it starts at about nine and finishes at six," Claire said, adding about two hours to the actual length of her conference. She felt like she might need some time to herself tomorrow, away from the O'Connells.

"Do you get lunch?" Paolo asked. "Could I come meet you?"

"Oh, I'd like that," Claire said. She realized suddenly that it was true; she would like to see him. Visiting his family was stressful, but she wasn't tired of Paolo.

"Me too," Paolo said, squeezing her shoulders gently. He kissed the top of her head. "So . . . can I come visit you in the four-poster bed tonight?"

"Are you kidding?" Claire asked, sitting up. "Your mother's probably going to be patrolling the halls after seeing that condom. Besides, I thought it was your grandmother's bed. Wouldn't she rise up and haunt us?"

Paolo laughed. "No, my grandmother lives in Teaneck with my grandfather."

Claire rolled her eyes. "Well, you still can't come visit me," she said. "And I'd better get back to my own room, anyway. Good night."

She stood up and then bent and kissed him casually. Paolo pulled himself into a sitting position and kissed her back. He put his hands on her face, and Claire felt a quick tremble in her stomach. She put her arms around his neck.

"Good night," Paolo said, breaking the kiss. He lay back down on the bed and began flipping through *Highlights* again.

The trembly feeling was still in Claire's stomach. She stared at Paolo. *How can you kiss me like that and then go back to reading a magazine!* she wanted to shout. *Don't you know what it does to me?*

But she only cleared her throat softly and said, "Good night."

Paolo looked up at her and smiled. She suddenly had the feeling that he knew exactly what his kisses did to her.

"Sleep tight," Paolo said.

She gave him a sour look and stepped out into the darkened hall, pulling his door shut behind her.

Her clogs rapped loudly against the wooden floor, and Claire quickly slipped them off. She was holding them in one hand and straightening her miniskirt

68

with the other when the bathroom door opened and caught her in a wedge of light.

Claire looked up.

Mr. O'Connell was standing in the bathroom doorway, wearing a robe. He look at Claire, obviously taking in the removed shoes, the rumpled skirt, her flushed cheeks, and the incriminating stance outside Paolo's room. He grinned broadly and gave Claire a thumbs-up sign.

Claire managed to smile faintly and watched him as he disappeared down the hall. She closed her eyes and leaned against the wall. This was going to be a very long weekend.

Transcript of Zoey's First Interview

ZP: Testing, one, two, three . . . Okay, I'm about to interview Elmer Westin, third mate on the *Carolina*. I hope this tape recorder works.

        [Sound of doorbell]

EW: Hello?

ZP: Hello, Mr. Westin, I'm Zoey Passmore; I called to interview you about—

EW: Of course! Well, aren't you a pretty little thing.

ZP: *[Pause]* Well, thank you. I—may I come in?

EW: Sure! Sure! What did the shoe salesman with the lisp say to the housewife?

ZP: *[Startled]* I don't know.

EW: Let me come in and I'll look up your thize. *[Laughs]*

ZP: *[Briskly]* Well, where shall I sit?

EW: Right here on the couch next to me.

ZP: Actually I think I'd be more comfortable in this chair.

EW: No, no, sit next to me; I'm hard of hearing.

ZP: Well, all right. Let me just get my note–book. . . .

  [Sound of papers rustling, followed by silence]

ZP: Mr. Westin, if you don't get your hand off my leg in one second, you are going to be very sorry.

EW: Ouch!

ZP: I warned you! *[Into tape recorder]* Interview concluded!

Transcript of Zoey's Second Interview

ZP: Okay, testing, whatever, I'm about to interview John Littleton, watch officer on the *Carolina*.

[*Sound of doorbell*]

JL: Hello?

ZP: Mr. Littleton?

JL: Yes?

ZP: I'm Zoey Passmore and—

JL: Well, how do you do, Zoey. It's not every day I'm visited by pretty young ladies.

ZP: I have a black belt in karate.

JL: [*Puzzled*] Well, good for you! Would you like to come in?

ZP: Oh, yes, thank you.

JL: Would you like a cup of tea?

ZP: No, thanks, I'd rather—

JL: You really are just lovely. Do you have a boyfriend?

ZP: Mr. Littleton—

JL: Because if you don't, I'll introduce you to my grandson. Would you like to see his picture?

ZP: No, I—

JL: It's no trouble. The photo album's right here.

[*Sound of things being moved around*]

JL: There he is.

ZP: *He's a little kid!*

JL: He's not; he's twelve.

ZP: But I'm eighteen!

JL: Oh, I see. Well, in that case, what about my

	nephew? He's twenty-two. [*Sound of pages turning*] There he is at a barbecue last summer.
ZP:	[*Interested*] Oh, my, how old did you say he was?
JL:	Twenty-two.
ZP:	Single?
JL:	Yes, and—
ZP:	[*Regaining control*] Actually, Mr. Littleton, I'd really like to get started with our interview.
JL:	What interview?
ZP:	The interview that I called about? About the *Carolina.*
JL:	Oh, you have the wrong Mr. Littleton. You want my brother.
ZP:	[*Desperately*] Does he live here?
JL:	Oh, yeah—well, normally. Right now he's in Florida, though.
ZP:	Oh, for heaven's sake!
JL:	Sure you don't want that cup of tea? Hey, miss, come back. . . .

Nine

The next morning Nina gripped the steering wheel so tightly, her knuckles were white.

"Now, Nina," Mr. Samuels said, having given up any pretense of calling them Ms. Geiger and Ms. Passmore. "Just relax. All you have to do is drive us in some nice, easy figure eights around the traffic cones while I ask you a few test questions."

"But how can I drive and answer at the same time?" Nina asked anxiously.

"Well, that's what I'm trying to teach you," Mr. Samuels said, taking a sip of coffee. "You need to learn how to concentrate on your driving and your surroundings. We'll go nice and slow. Don't worry."

"What am I supposed to do?" Zoey asked from the backseat.

Mr. Samuels tossed her a test booklet. "You can study for when it's your turn."

"But I can't read while the car's in motion," Zoey protested. "I'll get carsick and throw up."

"And that would ruin the beautiful cashmere sweater she spent all her birthday money on," Nina informed Mr. Samuels.

Zoey gave her a murderous look, but Nina barely saw it. Her mind had slipped suddenly into the past, to a bright spring day when she helped Zoey pick out that sweater and the saleslady hadn't let them share a dressing room and they had burned in united righteous anger at the suspicious natures of grownups.

"Nina?" Mr. Samuels asked.

"Hmmm?"

"Are you ready?"

"I guess so." She took a deep breath.

"Okay," Mr. Samuels said. "Begin your first figure eight."

Nina put the car in gear and drove forward cautiously.

Mr. Samuels rustled the papers in his lap. "All right," he said. "Here's your first question. If two cars meet on a narrow grade and they can't pass, the right-of-way should be given to—"

"Me," Nina answered uncertainly.

"This is multiple choice," Mr. Samuels said wryly. "*(a)* neither car; *(b)* the car going uphill; *(c)* the car going downhill."

"Oh, gosh, *I* don't know," Nina said, steering carefully around the traffic cones. "Won't one of them eventually stick their hands out the car window and wave the other one through?"

"This is going to be longest day of your career," Zoey said to Mr. Samuels.

"Shut up!" Nina snapped. *"C! I guess c!"*

Mr. Samuels marked down her answer. "Okay. You may cross over a double line on the road to pass another car if it is *(a)* solid white; *(b)* solid yellow—"

"What on earth does the color of the car have to do with anything?" Nina asked, exasperated. A traffic cone disappeared under the right wheel.

"The line, Nina," Mr. Samuels said. "The color of the *line*."

"Oh. Solid yellow."

"I haven't given you all the choices yet," Mr. Samuels said, sighing.

"Well, let's skip that one," Nina said. "Because I never pass anyone, anyway."

"No, you just run into them," Zoey said.

"Oh, very funny," Nina said, trying to glare at Zoey over her shoulder.

"Eyes on the road," Mr. Samuels said as Nina heard another traffic cone crunch beneath them.

"I'm looking, I'm looking," Nina muttered. "What's the next question?"

Mr. Samuels adjusted his half-moon glasses. "You must always look carefully for bicycles before you change lanes because *(a)* they don't have the right-of-way; *(b)* they're driven too fast; *(c)* they are hard to see."

"*D*," Nina answered. "We're bigger than they are."

Mr. Samuels groaned.

"Hey," Zoey said suddenly, "Nina's squashed all the cones. She's driving around flat orange circles!"

"Shut up, criminal," Nina snarled.

"Criminal?" Zoey said. "I'm not a criminal."

"What do you call speeding?" Nina asked, practically shouting. "A crime! That's what it is, a crime!"

"Girls—," Mr. Samuels tried to interject.

"Well, what do you call a car accident?" Zoey countered. "A good deed?"

"A traffic violation," Nina said bitingly. "A mere traffic violation."

"Girls," Mr. Samuels said again. "If you don't stop this bickering, I'm not going to pass either one of you."

"Oh, come on," Nina said. "You're not going to pass us, *anyway*."

Aisha stayed in bed and faked being asleep while she heard Felicia getting ready. She didn't want Felicia to have another chance to talk about her "discussion" with Christopher. Instead Aisha kept her eyes closed and concentrated on taking deep, even breaths.

She heard Felicia put something on her nightstand—paper by the sound of it—and then walk out quietly, shutting the door behind her. Aisha rolled over and opened her eyes.

There was a note on her nightstand.

Dear Aisha,
   Have a good weekend. Say hi to Christopher for me! F.

Aisha crumpled the note into a ball and got out of bed. She threw the note into the wastebasket and then went to the door and stuck her head out into the hall. No sign of Felicia.

She closed the door, locked it, and fastened the safety chain. Then she turned to Felicia's desk. *I don't think I'm going to like myself very much for this,* Aisha thought. *But I have to know. Remember that phone bill?* She shuddered, remembering how she had discovered that Felicia had made eleven calls to Christopher while Aisha had been out of the room. The calls had only been a few seconds long— like Felicia had gotten the answering machine and hung up—but it disturbed Aisha to know that she had even made them.

She opened the top drawer, quickly memorized

the order of things, and removed the first object. An address book.

Aisha flipped through it. It was full of the names and addresses of people, mostly in Boston. Aisha checked under *C* and *S,* but Christopher's number wasn't in there.

Maybe she has him listed under some other name, Aisha thought. *Some code or something.*

She turned back to the beginning and began going through the numbers more slowly, searching for the North Harbor area code. Abruptly she closed the book impatiently. If Felicia wanted Christopher's number, she could get it out of Aisha's own address book, which lay trustingly open on top of her desk.

Aisha's mouth twisted wryly. *Of course, I don't think very highly of people who snoop through other people's belongings,* she thought.

She put the address book back and removed the object below it: Felicia's checkbook. Aisha skimmed it with a minimum of interest. She didn't really expect to see anything incriminating. It didn't seem likely that Felicia would write "Sexy underwear for weekend with Christopher" under the Description of Transaction heading.

She put the checkbook back. Blank stationery and envelopes filled the rest of the drawer. Aisha closed it and opened the second one. Well, this looked a little more promising. A small decorated metal box filled with hard candies and one photograph.

The photograph was of Felicia and a boy Aisha had never seen. The boy was very handsome, tanned, and muscular. His arms were wrapped around Felicia from the back, and he looked straight into the camera. The picture had been taken outdoors, and a few strands of Felicia's hair blew across his face. Felicia was wearing a swimsuit, and her head was thrown back in laughter. She looked so happy that Aisha hardly recognized her.

Aisha flipped the picture over, but there was nothing written on the back—no date or anything. But it must be a fairly recent picture because Felicia looked about the same as she did now. Aisha put the picture back.

Next to the metal box was a stack of greeting cards. Aisha took them out. The one on top was a birthday card. She tried to remember when Felicia's birthday was but couldn't. She opened the card. It was just signed "*XOXO*, Dad."

Aisha flipped through the rest of the cards but couldn't find anything that wasn't from Felicia's parents or her friend Gaby. She put the cards back.

There was only one more drawer left, and when Aisha pulled it out, she saw it was filled with notebooks. She sighed and closed the drawer.

She turned to the dresser and opened the top drawer. The top three drawers were Felicia's, of course. She'd moved into the room first.

Aisha ran her hand quickly and lightly under the neatly folded sweaters. Nothing. She opened the next drawer and did the same—and her hand closed over a hard shape. Aisha withdrew a small book with a flowered cloth cover. She knew what it was as surely as if the words were stamped on the front: Felicia's diary.

Aisha did not open it. *I am not that kind of person,* she told herself. *I do have standards, thank you. I might paw through her old birthday cards, but I don't read other people's diaries. How would I feel if she read mine?*

But she was dying to read it. Aisha bit her lip. Then she quickly replaced the diary and shut the drawer.

This is so stupid, she thought. *Because even if I don't trust Felicia, I trust Christopher. Don't I? Don't I?*

And just then she heard Christopher's voice in the hall, talking to the resident assistant. "No, I don't need any help, thank you," he was saying. "I'm just looking for my fiancé."

The sound of his voice made Aisha's heart swell. She ran to the door, undid the chain, threw it open, and jumped into Christopher's arms like a stripper jumping out of a wedding cake—a lot like a stripper, actually, considering she was only wearing satin shortie pajamas.

LUCAS

Since every girl I've ever known has complained that construction workers whistle at them and/or make gross remarks, I decided to keep my own records. And you know what? In just one week I found out that girls are absolutely right.

<u>Girl</u>   <u>Number of Whistles/Remarks</u>

Kendra   ~~IIII~~ II
Nina   ~~IIII~~ ~~IIII~~ III
Holly McRoyAn   ~~IIII~~ II
Janelle   III
Sara Kendall   ~~IIII~~ ~~IIII~~
Marcy Woodard   ~~IIII~~
Zoey   ~~IIII~~ ~~IIII~~ ~~IIII~~ ~~IIII~~ ~~IIII~~ ~~IIII~~ III
My mother(!) I

And yes, my mother was all alone on the street,

so I know it was her they were whistling at.

And also yes, I was personally responsible for ~~IIII~~ ~~IIII~~ ~~IIII~~ ~~IIII~~ ~~IIII~~ of the whistles at Zoey.

Ten

Zoey studied the driving range in front of her. It didn't look too bad, basically just a big loop track with different-colored lines and markings.

"All right, Zoey," Mr. Samuels said. "We're going to do some braking exercises."

"I think I feel a case of whiplash coming on," Nina said cheerfully.

"Why do I have to do braking exercises?" Zoey asked. "*She's* the one who keeps rear-ending people."

"Nina will have to do this, too," Mr. Samuels said. "Now, see those red lines? I want you to go around the track once, take our speed up to thirty-five miles an hour, and then stop at the red line when you come to it."

Zoey bit her lip.

"At thirty-five miles an hour," Mr. Samuels continued, "the average stopping distance is about a hundred feet. So you're going to have to be the judge of when we're a hundred feet from the red line and begin to brake then."

"She's going to be just horrible at this," Nina informed Mr. Samuels. "She can't even estimate how much a *tablespoon* is—"

"I can't concentrate with her eating those Cheetos so loudly back there," Zoey interrupted. "It's like having a horse crunching up an apple in my ear."

"Nina, chew with your mouth closed," Mr. Samuels said automatically.

"I *am* chewing with my mouth closed," Nina said indignantly. "I wasn't raised in a barn, you know. And if you don't make me put the Cheetos away, I'll give you some."

"Deal," Mr. Samuels said, cupping his hands. Nina leaned forward and poured out some Cheetos.

"You're playing favorites," Zoey said reproachfully.

"No, I'm not," Mr. Samuels said, crunching. "It's impossible to play favorites when I don't like either of you. Now, please start the exercise."

"Is there an air bag back here?" Nina asked.

Zoey ignored her and put the car in gear.

"Okay," Mr. Samuels said, watching the speedometer. "Now, don't ride the brake."

"What does that mean?" Zoey asked.

"It means, don't keep your left foot on the brake and your right foot on the gas," Mr. Samuels said. "Use your right foot for everything."

"She likes to be prepared," Nina said. "In case she sees a child or elderly person, she can really accelerate."

"Shut up," Zoey said, tensing. She saw the red line and braked. The car drew to a slightly shuddering stop.

"I'll just measure how you did," Mr. Samuels said, opening his door.

"You're going to need a really long tape measure," Nina said. "Because I can see the red line way, way behind us."

Zoey rolled her eyes. "Can we stuff a sock in her mouth?" she asked Mr. Samuels.

"Believe me," he said, "nothing would give me more pleasure. However, in this instance she happens to be right. Drive around and try it one more time."

Nina grinned broadly in the rearview mirror. "Do you want me to pace it off?" she offered.

"Thank you, Nina, but that won't be necessary," Mr. Samuels said. "Try again, Zoey, and this time don't pump the brake so much."

"No kidding," Nina said. "It felt like you had a cramp and—"

"Shut up!" Zoey shouted, hitting the steering wheel with her fist. "Just shut up!"

"No!" Nina shouted back. "You wouldn't be quiet when I was driving, so I'm not going to be quiet while *you're*—"

"I'm warning you—"

"You're warning me!" Nina shouted. "What are you going to do? Scare me with more of your so-called driving?"

"Don't tempt me! I'll—"

"Girls!" Mr. Samuels thundered. "Silence. Right. This. Minute."

Zoey breathed heavily, staring out the window, her jaw pushed forward.

"That's it," Mr. Samuels said. "That's the last straw. I'm separating you. The two of you will complete the rest of this lesson privately."

Nina rolled down her window and stared out at nothing.

Mr. Samuels sighed and shook his head.

Zoey sat back, feeling oddly hollow. *How*

strange, she thought. *It's almost—almost like I'm disappointed.*

It was very bewildering.

The October wind made Nina's hair look even spikier than usual as she leaned against the ferry railing, talking to Lucas.

"So all I can say," she said, "is that I hope Zoey gets a blood blister from pounding the wheel like that because it was really, really immature."

Lucas opened his mouth to say something, but she rushed on breathlessly. "And then during the braking exercise Mr. Samuels had the nerve to say that I was no judge of distance, and I said that he was no judge of character, and things really deteriorated from there. It's been one of the worst days of my life, practically. But how are you? That's great news, by the way, about Zoey bringing you that sandwich."

"I thought you were wishing blood blisters on her," Lucas said.

"Well, yes," Nina admitted. "But nothing serious."

"And anyway," Lucas said. "That sandwich was all Adam's idea."

Nina frowned. "Who's Adam?"

"Some long lost relative of theirs," Lucas said bitterly. "He's helping out at the restaurant."

"Oh, that handsome guy?" Nina asked.

"You think he's handsome?" Lucas asked.

Nina winced at the hurt on his face and said hastily, "Well, only if you go for that type."

"What type?" Lucas asked sourly. "The handsome type?"

"The, um, slick, insincere type," Nina said. "Which I don't go for. And neither does Zoey. No one goes for that type. Adam's probably a really lonely individual."

Mercifully Lucas interrupted her to say, "Some little boy is waving at you."

"Really? Where?" Nina asked, squinting. "Oh, no, that's not a little boy, that's Julius McMartin. I wonder what he's going to North Harbor for?"

"Who's Julius McMartin?" Lucas asked.

"He's this genius in my calculus class," Nina said. "He's actually older than he looks, but not by much. Gosh, he won't stop waving—I'd better go say hello."

Reluctantly she crossed the deck to where Julius was standing, all bundled up in a thermal coat with a hood.

"Hi, Nina!" he said, bouncing up and down on the balls of his feet.

Nina wondered whether he was cold or had to go to the bathroom or what.

"Hi, Julius," she said. "What brings you to North Harbor?"

"I'm going to eat at Passmores'," Julius said. "I hear they do a wonderful chicken Alfredo."

"Oh, well, yes. They do," Nina said.

"Do you know anyone who works there?" Julius asked excitedly. "Do you want me to say hello for you?"

Nina had a fleeting image of Julius standing at the counter, his glasses fogged, saying *Nina sends her regards!* to Benjamin.

"No," she said. "I used to know the people who work there, but I don't anymore—Julius, *why* are you bouncing up and down like that?"

"Because I'm so excited to see you!" Julius burst out. "Because that was a big lie about going to Pass-mores'. I've really been riding this ferry all day, hoping to see you. And here you are!"

"Julius," Nina said uncertainly. "Why would you ride—"

"Because I'm in love with you!" Julius sang out. Nina prayed that no one was close enough to hear. "Ever since that day when Mr. Robinson made you go to the board and do that problem and you got all flustered and he still wouldn't let you sit down, I've just been totally in love with you."

"Well, I'm in this kind of crazy situation—," Nina began.

"And I've made up a million reasons to go to the office," Julius continued. "I keep saying that I need to see my career counselor because I can't decide about early acceptance at Yale, but really I decided a long time ago, and it's all been a big ruse just to catch a glimpse of you."

"Well," Nina said since he was looking at her so expectantly. "Well. I don't know what to say."

Julius opened his mouth, and Nina had the awful feeling that he was going to tell her what to say, but at just that moment the ferry pulled into the landing. "Oh, well, I'd better go—there's my boyfriend; I'll see you later," she said rapidly, and ran off to catch up to Lucas.

"Oh, my God," she moaned, clutching Lucas's arm. "This really is the worst day of my life. Julius McMartin is in love with me."

Lucas glanced back. "Yeah, he's staring after you with this big smile on his face."

Nina groaned. "I can't look," she said. "I just can't. Do you think anyone overheard—"

She broke off suddenly.

Zoey was leaving the ferry, too.

She was on the same ferry with us, Nina thought. *Which means she saw me talking to Lucas and she probably saw me talking to Julius, too. Oh, I bet she's just so happy about what a loser I am.*

"Hello, Lucas," Zoey said softly.

"Hello," Lucas said.

Zoey walked on ahead of them. Nina noticed that Lucas followed her with his eyes.

"Did you see that?" Nina said indignantly. "See how much she hates me? She didn't even *speak* to me."

"True," Lucas said. "But then, you didn't speak to her either."

Champion Traffic School
Practical Driving Evaluation

Instructor: H. R. Samuels
Student: Zoey Passmore
Target test time: 35 min.
Test completed in: 25 min.

Maneuvers

Emergency stop	Good	Fair	**(Poor)**
Three-point turn	Good	**(Fair)**	Poor
Corner reverse	Good	Fair	**(Poor)**
Parallel parking	Good	Fair	**(Poor)**
Hill start	**(Good)**	Fair	Poor
Angle start	**(Good)**	Fair	Poor

Form

Hands crossed while steering	Always	Sometimes	**(Never)**
Allowed wheel to spin back	**(Always)**	Sometimes	Never
Use of mirrors	**(Always)**	Sometimes	Never

Errors

Total number of errors: 21
Errors that created actual or potential danger to other road users: 9
Number of times instructor applied emergency brake: 8

Comments:

Number of times student checked lipstick in the rearview mirror: 19.

Champion Traffic School
Practical Driving Evaluation

Instructor: H. R. Samuels
Student: Nina Geiger
Target test time: 35 min.
Test completed in: 90 min.

Maneuvers

Emergency stop	Good	Fair	**(Poor)**
Three-point turn	Good	Fair	**(Poor)**
Corner reverse	Good	**(Fair)**	Poor
Parallel parking	Good	**(Fair)**	Poor
Hill start	**(Good)**	Fair	Poor
Angle start	Good	Fair	**(Poor)**

Form

Hands crossed while steering	**(Always)**	Sometimes	Never
Allowed wheel to spin back	Always	Sometimes	**(Never)**
Use of mirrors	Always	Sometimes	**(Never)**

Errors

Total number of errors: 24
Errors that created actual or potential danger to other road users: 6
Number of times instructor applied emergency brake: 5

Comments:

Student climbed into a car and remarked, "Now, which one is the gas again?" Claimed to be joking.

Eleven

Aisha was having such a good time with Christopher that she was almost sorry she'd agreed to meet Graham and his girlfriend for dinner. Gazing at Christopher's profile as they walked along Prescott Street, Aisha thought that she would be perfectly happy if they spent the rest of their lives on a desert island together and never saw anyone else again.

Christopher must have been feeling the same way because he suddenly squeezed her hand and said, "Let's stop and have a cup of coffee before we go to the restaurant, okay? Just the two of us?"

"Okay," Aisha agreed happily. "But I don't know anyplace around here."

"How about this place?" Christopher asked. "The Oak?"

Aisha nodded and followed him into the coffeehouse.

It was crowded, and they had to sit at the counter. Aisha perched on a stool awkwardly. She was wearing lined flannel slacks, and they were so slippery that she feared she might slide right off the stool at any moment. With the slacks she was wearing a champagne-colored silk blouse, and she had gathered her hair up in back in a complicated style. She was just wondering if she looked okay or if she looked like someone who was trying too hard when Christopher finished ordering their coffee and turned toward her.

He looked at her for a moment and then touched her face gently. "You are so *pretty*."

Aisha smiled, thinking that no one but Christopher could make a simple word like *pretty* sound so meaningful.

"Thanks," she said softly.

Their drinks arrived, and Christopher raised his glass. "To weekends in Boston," he said.

Aisha raised her glass, too, and took a sip, but she almost choked when Christopher suddenly said, "Hey, there's Felicia."

Aisha turned and looked. Yes, there was the familiar face and pale gold hair. Felicia hesitated and then waved. Christopher waved back, and after another hesitation Felicia began crossing the room toward them.

"Hi, guys," Felicia said, standing before them, and for a moment Aisha felt too dismal to answer. Because Felicia looked sensational. She was wearing a plain white T-shirt and faded jeans, but the simple clothing outlined her perfect figure, and her corn silk hair hung halfway down her back in a heavy shining curtain. Aisha knew suddenly that her own hairstyle, pants, blouse, boots, earrings—everything was wrong, all wrong.

"Hi, Felicia," Christopher said.

"I thought you were going away," Aisha blurted rudely.

Felicia laughed. "I just left our room," she said. "I didn't leave town."

"Would you like something to drink?" Christopher asked.

"Oh, that'd be great," Felicia said. "Club soda, please."

Christopher turned to order for her, and Aisha tried to fight down a wave of jealousy. *Don't be so insecure,* she told herself. *If he bought a drink for Nina or Zoey or even Claire, you'd love him all the more for his generosity.*

"So where *are* you staying?" she asked Felicia.

Felicia shrugged. "At a girlfriend's apartment."

Now Aisha was irked on two counts. First of all, she had always disliked girls who used the word *girlfriend* to describe their female friends, as though they were different from male friends. Second, she had really been hoping that Felicia was staying with some guy because that would have made her seem less available than she seemed right now.

"So what have you guys been up to this weekend?" Felicia asked. "Seeing the sights?"

"No, just being together, mainly," Christopher said. He put his arm around Aisha, but she was too sulky to take any pleasure in it. "How about you?" Christopher asked. "How's your Saturday been?"

Felicia rolled her eyes. "Very stressful. I had to meet this professor for lunch, and as I was walking to the restaurant some weird man pulled up next to me and asked me where the Cottonwood Café was, and like an idiot, I said, 'Oh, it's right up here; I'm going there myself.' And then of course he followed me at about one mile an hour, and when we were in the restaurant, he gave me a big goofy smile and my professor was like, 'Do you *know* him?'"

Christopher laughed, and Aisha managed a smile.

I don't have lunch with professors, she thought. *Men don't follow me down the street. I never tell stories like that.*

Felicia checked her watch. "I'm supposed to meet some people here," she said. "I don't know what's keeping them."

"Well, actually," Aisha said, "we're supposed to meet some friends, too. We should probably be going."

"Will you be okay?" Christopher asked Felicia. "Should we stay until your friends get here?"

Oh, for God's sake, Aisha thought, irritated. *What do you think is going to happen to her in a coffee-house? Maybe a few strangers will propose matrimony, but that's about all I can think of.*

She suddenly realized that Felicia was watching her, and Aisha wondered what her face looked like.

"No," Felicia said, still looking at Aisha. "I'll be fine. Have a good time at dinner."

"We will," Christopher said as Aisha slipped into her jacket. "Have a good night."

"You too," Felicia said, smiling.

Aisha managed a wave and then followed Christopher out onto the street. He gave her a quick one-armed hug. "Now, where were we?"

Aisha didn't answer. *You were telling me how pretty I look,* she thought.

But suddenly, after seeing Felicia, she didn't feel pretty at all.

Zoey walked into the back room of the restaurant and tossed her tape recorder and notebook onto the desk. "Just give me a second to change, and I'll help set up for dinner," she said.

"That's okay; Benjamin and I have it under control," Adam said, "and your dad said he felt well enough to work the dinner shift, too."

Zoey felt self-conscious as her cousin looked her over thoughtfully. She was wearing brown flats, a long wool skirt, and a faded green cardigan. Her hair was so severely pulled back that no tendrils escaped to frame her face, and large glasses with tortoiseshell frames rested on her nose. "Where have you been?" Adam asked. "A librarian convention?"

"Oh, very funny," Zoey said, removing the glasses. She wasn't wearing any makeup. "I've been interviewing sailors who were on the *Carolina,* and yesterday one of them tried to put his hands on my leg and another one wants me to date his grandson."

Adam smiled. "And today?"

"Well, I thought dressing like this might make me seem a little more professional," Zoey said.

"Did it work?"

She sighed and sank into a chair. "No, today's sailor wanted me to clean his kitchen before he'd tell me anything."

"You're kidding!" Adam said, laughing.

"I know," Zoey said ruefully. "It was just like *The Karate Kid,* where that old man makes him wax the cars. But I would rather have waxed a car than cleaned this man's kitchen, which hadn't been cleaned since about 1948."

Adam stared at her. "You mean you actually did it? You cleaned his kitchen?"

"Of course I cleaned his kitchen!" Zoey said, exasperated. "I'm desperate for information. I even made him an omelette. And then finally he told me his big story and—get this—he was *asleep* when the ship went down and didn't wake up until they were rescued."

She sat back in her chair and sighed. "What am I going to do? My entire speech is going to consist of one sentence: On November 4, 1947, Nelson Rimsdale realized his socks were wet, and then rescue arrived."

Adam smiled sympathetically and leaned forward to take one of her hands. "Well, aren't there other survivors? Can't you interview them over the phone?"

"Oh, Adam, most of these men are so old, they don't even hear the phone ringing. And they all want to talk to me in person. One guy even wants me to charter a boat and take him out to the site of the wreck!" Zoey shook her head. "Besides, I think they all just want a little company. Most of them are so lonely, it makes me feel like crying—"

Zoey broke off, realizing that she was, in fact, very close to crying. She could feel her chin trembling, and her eyes were damp.

Adam's arms were around her in an instant. "Shhh," he said, kneeling in front of her chair. "It'll be okay. We'll think of something. Here, blow your nose." He handed Zoey a Kleenex.

She blew her nose obediently.

"What I think," Adam said, "is that you've been working too hard and you need some time off. How does going to a movie with your cousin sound?"

Zoey wiped her eyes and smiled shakily. "Actually it sounds kind of pathetic," she said. "Like this girl in my class who had to go to the prom with her uncle because no one asked her." But her blue eyes sparkled as she looked at Adam. "But since you're the cousin in question, I'd love to go."

Twelve

"So how did the conference go after lunch?" Paolo asked.

"Oh, fine," Claire said absently, jerking hot roller pins out of her hair. The rollers tumbled to the floor, but she didn't pick them up. "I'll tell you about it some other time. Right now I'm a lot more interested in what to wear."

"Oh, no," Paolo said in alarm, sitting upright on her bed. "No way am I playing that game with you."

"What game?" Claire asked, yanking open the closet door.

"The game where you ask me what to wear," Paolo said, "and I tell you and you say, *What are you, crazy? That makes me look fat!*"

Claire made a face. "Well, this is different," she said. "I really do need your help because this party is starting in five minutes and I have no idea what to wear."

Paolo smiled. "How about fishnet stockings and a Playboy Bunny tuxedo?"

"Paolo!" She threw a sock at him. "Will you be serious for once? I need to know what everyone else is going to be wearing."

"Are you kidding?" he said. "We're a half-Irish,

half-Spanish family. Fifty percent of the people will wear kilts, and the other half will dress like priests."

Claire was distractedly examining a black miniskirt. *Too dressy. You don't want to look too formal—remember the suit?* She tossed it aside. "Why?" she asked. "Is it a costume party?"

"Something like that."

"Paolo?" Mrs. O'Connell called. "Would you come give me a hand?"

"Be right there!" he shouted. He kissed Claire's forehead. "Look, wear whatever you want. You're going to be the most gorgeous girl there, I promise." He left the room.

Claire sighed in irritation. *I don't care if I'm gorgeous,* she thought. *I just want to fit in . . . although I'd like to be gorgeous, too.* Claire turned to face the closet, relieved that she had brought practically her entire wardrobe with her.

The doorbell rang downstairs, and she groaned. The first guests arriving. She quickly selected black jeans and a beautiful soft cherry red cashmere sweater.

The doorbell rang several more times, but by the time Claire left her bedroom ten minutes later, she felt confident that she'd made the right choice. The jeans emphasized her long legs, and the red sweater made her skin glow. She'd brushed her hair until it shone, and her makeup was perfect.

She descended the staircase, hoping to see Paolo, but instead she saw two men dressed as priests at the bottom of the stairs. Her eyes widened in surprise. So it really *was* a costume party!

"Damn Paolo!" she said aloud.

The priests turned instantly.

"May God forgive you," one of them said, smiling. He had dark hair and eyes that sparkled just like Paolo's. Claire would have bet he wasn't more than twenty-one.

"We're more into saving people than damning them," the other one said. He ran his eyes appreciatively over Claire. "But just out of curiosity, what has Paolo done now?"

She shook her head and descended the last few stairs until she was even with them. "He didn't tell me it was a costume party," she said. "Or rather he did tell me, but I didn't believe him because he jokes around so much. And then I come downstairs, and the first people I see are you two."

"But we really are priests," the dark-eyed one protested. "I'm Father Miguel, and this is Father Brendan."

Claire looked from one to the other. Father Brendan was blond, but his eyes twinkled as mischievously as Father Miguel's. "You aren't priests," she said, smiling.

Father Brendan pretended to be offended. "Why not? Don't we look holy, devout?"

"No," Claire said. "Not in the slightest. Besides, priests don't drink beer," she added to Father Miguel, gesturing to the bottle in his hand.

"They don't?" he said. "Hey, Brendan, we'd better call Bishop Mike. I think he was headed out to a three kegger tonight."

Claire rolled her eyes.

Father Brendan laughed. "Any other giveaways?" he asked.

"Well," Claire said smiling. "Priests don't give girls the once-over as they walk down the stairs. Or does Bishop Mike go to strip joints, too?"

"Maybe," Father Miguel said thoughtfully. "On Tuesdays. That's his day off."

"Priests don't have days off!" Claire protested, laughing.

Mrs. O'Connell came out of the kitchen. She was wearing white pants and a pretty raspberry-colored blouse. "Claire," she said, smiling. "I'm glad to see you met my nephews. Boys, this is Claire, Paolo's girlfriend. Claire, this is Father Miguel and Father Brendan."

"We've already had the pleasure," Father Brendan said. Father Miguel bowed slightly.

Claire felt as though there were a sharp stick caught in her throat. She coughed. "You mean," she said, "that they are actually priests?"

Mrs. O'Connell looked puzzled. "Well, of course."

Father Miguel and Father Brendan were grinning at her broadly.

Claire's jaw dropped practically to the floor. "Oh, my God," she said. "I mean, oh, wow."

Looking back, Aisha could pinpoint the exact moment she figured it out.

She had read somewhere once that mathematical geniuses could look at a complicated problem before going to bed and while they slept, their minds would do the work and supply them with the answer when they awoke. Like when Newton saw the apple fall out of the tree and the next morning woke up with gravity all figured out. Aisha didn't claim to be a genius, mathematical or otherwise, but it was later clear that during the time she had introduced Christopher to Graham and met Graham's girlfriend and made small talk and ordered dinner and laughed and smiled, her mind had been going over the facts and had arrived at the inevitable conclusion.

Christopher and Felicia had planned to meet at that coffeehouse.

That sentence popped into Aisha's mind just as she took a bite of garlic bread. She froze. Suddenly she couldn't swallow, and the rich buttery flavor of the garlic bread was sickening.

What was it Christopher had said earlier? *Let's stop and have a cup of coffee before we go to the restaurant, okay? Just the two of us . . . How about this place? The Oak?*

"Are you okay?" Graham's girlfriend asked suddenly. Her name was Cheryl and she was very pretty, with dark hair and freckles.

Aisha swallowed the piece of garlic bread. It felt like a wooden block. "Yes, I'm fine," she said. "Aren't you in my psychology class?"

But another part of her mind was hearing Felicia say, *I'm supposed to meet some people here. . . . I don't know what's keeping them. . . .*

What *had* been keeping them? The fact that they didn't exist at all? And since when did Felicia hang around waiting for friends? Aisha had never seen her so much as walk across campus by herself, let alone wait in a coffeehouse without a group of pals.

"North Harbor," Aisha heard herself respond, amazed that her mouth was able to carry on a conversation while her mind was occupied by something else entirely. "You've probably never heard of it. It's a tiny island off the coast of Maine." She was on autopilot.

"Oh, I used to go to Maine for summer vacation with some friends of my parents," Cheryl said.

And why had Felicia so conveniently cleared out of the dorm room this weekend when last weekend she had clung to them like flypaper? Well, Aisha knew the answer to that one: because Felicia and Christopher had planned it. But why? Was it really so that Christopher and Aisha could have some time alone together or—or—

Or was it to keep Aisha from seeing the sparks between Christopher and Felicia?

Why else would Felicia suddenly be playing the considerate roommate? It certainly didn't apply to any other part of her life. She still left her wet towels on the floor, she still borrowed Aisha's clothes without asking, she still drank Aisha's Snapple drinks and ate her Cocoa Pebbles and stole her hair scrunchies, so why was she so eager to leave this weekend?

And what about Christopher? Last weekend he had insisted that spending time with Felicia was the only way to improve matters, and now he and Felicia had been the ones to decide she should leave. There could only be one reason: They didn't want Aisha to see them together.

"Excuse me," Aisha said. "I have to go to the ladies' room."

"And I have to call my sister, Kendra," Christopher said, standing up. "We'll be right back."

Kendra? Aisha thought crazily. *Is that really who you're going to call?*

Christopher put his hand on the small of her back as they walked toward the back of the restaurant. "Graham is really cool," he said.

Aisha couldn't even respond. She only nodded and then turned and went quickly into the ladies' room.

She splashed cold water on her face and then leaned her forehead against the mirror.

Don't be paranoid, she told herself. *You'll ruin everything.* But suddenly she couldn't help it because she remembered something else, a conversation she'd had with Felicia earlier in the week.

Where are you and Christopher meeting Graham? We haven't decided yet.

Have you ever been to Sophie's? It's a great place.

Oh, thanks, maybe we'll give it a try. . . .

And here they were at Sophie's, which was so conveniently just down the street from The Oak. And Felicia had known they would be here. Had she also known that Christopher would steer them into The Oak? Had she known because Christopher had told her?

"I've got to stop thinking like this," Aisha whispered.

But she couldn't stop, any more than Newton could think the apple back onto the tree.

Thirteen

Claire went straight to the corner of the living room that Paolo's mother had set up as a bar.

"I'll have a glass of sherry," she said to the bartender.

He poured one for her, and she knocked it back in one long swallow.

The bartender gave her a lopsided grin. "Have another one," he said. "They're small."

"Thank you," Claire said, holding out her glass. She drank the second sherry, had the bartender top off her glass, took another sip, and headed off in search of Paolo.

She found him in the crowded kitchen, talking to Marta.

"How could you?" Claire asked, punching him on the shoulder.

"How could I what?" he asked, looking surprised but kind of pleased, as though whatever he had done was worth it to get her so riled up.

"Why didn't you warn me—*seriously* warn me—that there would be priests here?" Claire said.

"Paolo, you idiot," Marta moaned.

"What happened?" Paolo asked, laughing.

"It's not funny!" Claire hissed. "I accused Father Brendan and Father Miguel of being fakes."

Paolo threw back his head and laughed. Both Claire and Marta punched him.

"Listen, you dork," Marta said. "Claire's going to break up with you if you don't start protecting her—" She broke off suddenly, looking at Claire. "Do you feel okay?"

"Yes, I'm fine," Claire said, and frowned. It had sounded as though she'd said "yesh" instead of "yes." But surely she wasn't slurring her words. Not after two glasses of sherry. Two and a half.

"Anyway," Paolo said, having finally caught his breath. "I did warn you. I told you that half the people would dress as priests and half the people would wear kilts."

"You said *dress* as priests," Claire protested. "You didn't say they'd *be* priests!"

"Yes, and who wears kilts?" Marta asked. "We're not that weird."

"Uncle Niall," Paolo said.

Marta shrugged. "Well, okay, we are that weird," she said. She looked at Claire apologetically. "Sorry, but—"

They were interrupted by a loud Irish voice booming in the next room.

"Good Lord!" Marta said. "It's him." Mrs. O'Connell was walking past, and Marta grabbed her arm. "Mom, tell me that's not Uncle Niall."

Mrs. O'Connell smiled weakly. "I'm afraid it is."

Marta and Paolo moaned in unison. "*Mom,* I thought you said he couldn't come to our parties anymore," Marta said. "Not after last year when he wrote his name on the snowbank in urine."

Mrs. O'Connell pulled her arm out of Marta's grasp and straightened her blouse. "Well, sweetie," she said lamely. "He's family, and if we didn't have family to our parties, then—"

"We'd have much better parties," Paolo finished. "Oh, no, here he comes."

Claire glanced through the open kitchen doorway. A large man with a halo of fluffy white hair and a very red face stood in the living room, laughing and looking about. He saw them, and his face lit up. He began making his way through the crowd toward them.

Claire quickly downed the rest of her sherry.

"Paolo!" Uncle Niall said heartily, slapping Paolo on the back. He saluted Marta and dropped heavily into a kitchen chair. "Great party," he said to Mrs. O'Connell. "Although I may have to sleep in the guest room. I've had too much punch, I fear."

"How can you have had too much punch?" Marta said, exasperated. "You've been here five minutes."

"It happens, my dear lassie," Uncle Niall said, unruffled. His eyes settled on Claire. "Who's this lass?"

"Stop saying lass," Paolo said. "You're from Newark, not Ireland."

Lass, my ass, Claire thought, and giggled.

"This is Paolo's girlfriend, Claire Geiger," Marta said.

Everyone keeps introducing me as Paolo's girlfriend, Claire thought. *Everyone—except Paolo.*

"This is my uncle Niall," Paolo said.

"How do you do?" Claire said politely.

Uncle Niall laughed. "Are you the one who thought Brendan wasn't really a priest?" he asked.

"Shut up, Uncle Niall," Marta and Mrs. O'Connell said.

Uncle Niall ignored them. He leered at Claire. "Well, you're certainly lovely enough," he said. He patted his knee. "Don't you want to sit on my lap and make an old man happy?"

"Shut up, Uncle Niall!" Mrs. O'Connell said again.

Claire flushed, and Uncle Niall cackled. He made a gesture of mock courtesy. "How lovely to see a young virgin blush," he said.

At the word *virgin* the whole kitchen had mysteriously fallen quiet, and Claire could feel all eyes upon her. There was a beat of silence.

"Shut up, Uncle Niall!" the whole room screamed.

Claire had an instant of profound pleasure, realizing that the whole room was on her side, was coming to her defense. But it was only one second and then her tense, overwrought stomach rebelled against the sherry. She leaned over and threw up into the kitchen sink.

Zoey could barely keep her eyes open on the ferry ride home. She had been working at the restaurant so continuously that her body had only two modes: working and sleeping. She breathed in the crisp October air and tried to wake up.

"Did you have a good time?" Adam asked from beside her.

"Oh, yes," Zoey said, smiling at him gratefully. "It's been so long since I've to a movie that I could hardly believe they were still making them. Whenever an actor walked on-screen, I kept thinking, *What's he doing here? Hasn't he retired?*"

Adam laughed. "Come on, it can't have been that long."

"No, I guess not," Zoey admitted. "But it sure seems like it. Sometimes I have dreams that I'm setting the tables at the restaurant over and over, and then the alarm goes off, and I know I have to get up and go set the tables at the restaurant." She sighed. "It's so unending. I don't know how my parents have done it for so many years."

"Speaking of your parents," Adam said, "when does your mom get out of the hospital?"

Zoey drew her coat more tightly around her. "Pretty soon," she said. "We haven't been visiting her that much because it means asking Christopher or Kendra to cover for us, but now that my dad's not so tired all the time and you're here—"

She broke off suddenly, looking contrite.

Adam laughed and put his arm around her. "Stop looking so guilty," he said. "I know you're thinking that you should have gone to the hospital instead of to a movie with me—"

"How did you know that?" Zoey asked, surprised.

"Because your face is such an open book," Adam said gently. Zoey couldn't help noticing how long his eyelashes were. "Anyway, tomorrow you can go visit your mom, but tonight you deserved a break."

"Well, I do feel much better," Zoey said, leaning against him. "I'm ready to go back out and tackle the world of lecherous old sailors."

"Good girl," Adam said. He rubbed a hand up her arm. "Are you cold?"

"A little," Zoey said. The way he was looking at her put a slight flutter in her stomach.

"Do you want to go inside?"

"No," she said. "I like it better out here."

A boy in a fur-lined parka walked by and glanced at them.

"Who *is* that guy?" Adam asked. "He's always on this ferry."

Zoey giggled. "I don't know his name, but I found out today that he has a horrible crush on an island girl, and he's been riding the ferry endlessly hoping to see her. He's going to get stuck on the island overnight if he isn't careful."

Adam shook his head. "Does the girl want to go out with him?"

"Are you kidding?" Zoey said. "Someone told me he's this, like, thirteen-year-old genius."

"So?" Adam said. "Maybe he's nice." He looked faintly disapproving. "That's so unfair."

Well, of course it's unfair, Zoey thought. *The whole popular-unpopular thing is unfair, but what can you do? Does he really think Nina dating a short brainiac is going to solve the world's problems?*

"I didn't say he wasn't nice," Zoey pointed out. "I'm just saying that Nina's not going to go for a big math nerd, that's all."

"Who's Nina?"

This was a perfectly reasonable question, but for a moment Zoey was shocked. What did he mean, "Who's Nina?" Nina was Nina. Everyone knew her; everyone admired her sense of humor and deplored her sense of style. How strange that someone could not know Nina.

But Zoey had met dozens of people at Berkeley who didn't know Nina. Why should it suddenly strike her as so strange? Why did she want Adam to understand—without being told—about Nina and who she would and wouldn't date and her history and how impossible she could be but how she had once made Zoey laugh so hard that the Coke she was drinking came out her nostrils?

"Zoey?" Adam asked, puzzled. "What is it?"

Zoey looked at him. "What is what?"

"You look so . . . I don't know. Distressed," Adam said.

"I was just remembering something," Zoey said. She smiled at him. "Nothing important."

"Are you sure?" Adam asked, putting his other arm around her.

He's going to kiss me, Zoey thought without surprise.

"Very sure," she whispered, and before he could even bend down to kiss her, she leaned up and pressed her mouth to his.

Zoey hadn't kissed anyone in even longer than she had been to the movies. It was as wonderful as she remembered.

Lucas rode in the enclosed deck of the ferry, something he'd never done in high school. Now when he rode outside, the salt and wind reopened the hundreds of tiny cuts on his hands.

He leaned his forehead against the glass and wondered why he was wasting his time working on Zoey's house. Tonight, for example, he'd gone all the way into Weymouth for supplies. Why? It didn't seem to make Zoey forgive him. So why didn't he forget the whole thing and spend what little free time he had sleeping, like a normal person?

Lucas shook his head. He couldn't quit the house now. He was addicted to it. He *liked* working on it, the same as he liked working on the lighthouse. Lucas sighed.

At that moment he happened to glance out the window and see Zoey's cousin. What was his name? Adam.

What was he doing here? Wasn't the whole point that he was going to help out at the restaurant? So what was he doing on the last ferry on Saturday night?

Lucas squinted. Kissing some girl, by the looks of it. His spirits rose a little. Well, that was one less thing to worry about. He didn't have to be jealous—

Adam turned slightly, and Lucas saw that the girl Adam was kissing was Zoey. And in the split second before his mind was swamped with jealousy, he managed to notice two things. That Zoey looked lovelier than he'd seen her look in weeks—and happier.

Nina

A strange thing happened today while I was reading to Benjamin. My mind began wandering (this isn't the strange part) and I was just sort of reading along automatically when I began feeling really aware of Benjamin lying on the bed.

I began wishing that I could lie on the bed next to him and put my arms around him and make the time go faster for him that way instead of blathering on like a human Books on Tape. And I wondered if I did lie on the bed next to him, what Benjamin would say, and

if that would make his four
hours go faster, and if maybe
it would even be the best
four hours of his whole day...

So then I hear Benjamin say,
"Nina? What's wrong? You've
stopped reading."

I said, "I did?"

And he said, "Yes, you said,
'I wish...,' and then you were
quiet for a long time."

Thank God I didn't say anything else! Or did I? What if
Benjamin's only being polite and
I really said the whole thing
out loud? Maybe I shouldn't
read to him anymore. But I
couldn't bear to give it up.

Fourteen

No doubt about it: Aisha was pissed. Christopher just didn't know why.

They were saying good-bye in the bright and crowded dorm lobby because, Aisha said, she had to go to the library and study as soon as Christopher left. Christopher thought her tone implied, *And the sooner you leave, the better.*

"So," he said, touching her hair. "Now that Adam's helping at the restaurant, I could probably come back next weekend."

"No," Aisha said, moving her head so that his hand no longer touched her. "I have a lot of exams and stuff coming up."

"I see," Christopher said. "Well, that's cool. I understand."

She gave him a tight smile. "Thanks for your permission."

"I didn't mean it like—"

"I know," she said quickly. "I'm sorry if I sounded witchy."

"It's okay," Christopher said. He hesitated. "Is something bothering you?"

"No." Her voice was like a door slamming.

For the hundredth time Christopher reviewed the

weekend in his mind. Aisha had seemed happy to see him. They had had a wonderful Saturday afternoon. Everything had seemed fine—right up until about the time they'd met Graham for dinner.

Christopher felt a twisting in his stomach. Could Aisha's mood have something to do with *Graham* . . . or with meeting Graham's girlfriend? Had she been jealous? Christopher's lips tightened. He didn't want to think that.

"Well, then . . ." He sighed and stuck his hands in his pockets. He wished he could hold Aisha's hand, but her arms were so full of books that he didn't know how the hell he was going to hug her goodbye. "I should probably be going."

"Thanks for coming," Aisha said in a weird voice, as though he were the telephone repairman.

"Eesh—," he began again, but just then a voice interrupted cheerily.

"Hi, Christopher; hi, Aisha," Felicia said, breezing past them. She had on a backpack, and her blond hair was covered by a baseball cap. She winked at Christopher. "See you later."

Christopher felt queasy when he saw the wink. It made him remember the phone call and that stupid sex quiz. For a second he wondered if Aisha had somehow found out about that, but he didn't think so. The timing wasn't right. Or was it? His eyes followed Felicia for a second. They'd seen Felicia right about the time Aisha had sunk into such a dark mood. But Felicia had been such a good sport this weekend, clearing out of the room and everything. *No,* Christopher decided, *it probably had to do with Graham.*

He turned back to Aisha, but her eyes were still on Felicia, who stood waiting for the elevator, and her face was one of the unhappiest he had ever seen.

The guest room was already bright with sunshine by the time Claire heard someone set a glass on her nightstand. She opened one eye and saw Paolo grinning at her, and it all came back: drinking the sherry, barfing in the sink, being helped upstairs, passing out.

She groaned and pulled the pillow over her head.

"Are you going to be okay?" Paolo asked. "Or should I get Father Miguel to come up and administer the last rites?"

"How can you joke like that?" Claire asked irritably. She started to sit up, but a bolt of pain shot through her temples, and she lowered her head back to the pillow. "I'm so mortified, I could kill myself."

"Oh, don't worry," Paolo said. "Everyone was out of control last night. Even the priests got drunk and pushed over the gazebo."

"Paolo," Claire said, *"I threw up in your mother's kitchen sink."*

"I know," Paolo said. He sat on the edge of the bed and held her hand. "But it wasn't so bad. She just used that sprayer thing and washed it all down the disposal."

Claire groaned again. "I think I could have done without that particular detail," she said.

"Have some juice," Paolo said. "You'll feel better."

Claire reached for the glass of orange juice and saw that she was still wearing the red cashmere sweater. The sleeve was now flecked with brown specks she didn't want to analyze very closely. Paolo looked maddeningly fresh and clean in jeans and an old Yale sweatshirt.

She drank the orange juice in one swallow. "Thanks," she said, handing the glass to Paolo.

"Do you feel up to breakfast?" Paolo asked. "My mother's making eggs and bacon for everyone who has a hangover, including both Fathers Miguel and Brendan, and Uncle Niall."

"They're still here?" Claire asked. Then she held up her hand. "Never mind, I don't even want to know. But if you think I can ever face your mother again after last night, you're crazy."

"Why not?" Paolo asked. "My mom likes you. She said so."

"What did she say?" Claire challenged. "I like a girl who has no inhibitions?"

"No, she said that she thought you were doing your best in a difficult situation," Paolo said.

"That is hardly the same thing as saying she *liked* me," Claire said. She made a noise as she thought of last night again. "Does this kind of thing happen every time you bring a girl home?"

Paolo was silent for a minute, stroking her hand. She glanced at him, but he seemed thoughtful. "I never brought a girl home before," he said. "I never wanted to."

Claire was touched. She studied his face but didn't see any of the teasing she normally found there. She squeezed his hand. "I think I'd like to take a shower," she said softly. "There's pieces of wilted lettuce in my hair."

Paolo nodded. "That's probably not all you'll find," he said, grinning. "The sink was kind of gross even *before* you put your head into it."

Claire rolled her eyes. She swung her legs onto the floor. "I'll meet you downstairs, okay?"

"Okay," Paolo said cheerfully. "Take your time."

Claire watched him as he left the room. Then she quickly gathered her clothes together and stuffed them into her suitcase. She went out into the hall and leaned over the banister. She could hear loud happy voices in the dining room, and the smell of bacon made her feel almost faint with hunger. But nobody was in the front hall.

She tiptoed down the stairs, the suitcase pressed against her leg, and eased open the front door, pausing for a moment to make sure there was no break in the jovial conversation from the next room. Satisfied, she shut it quietly behind her.

Her footsteps sounded loud on the gravel driveway, but she didn't look back. She threw her suitcase into the passenger seat of the car she had rented with Paolo and climbed in after it. She was on the way to North Harbor a minute later.

Nina

Well, isn't this typical?
It's like something out of a
bad novel: Two new guys arrive
on the island. One is tall, broad
shouldered, hazel eyed, a myste-
rious loner. He falls for an
island girl. Her name is Zoey.

Another guy arrives on the
island. He is short, nearsighted,
nerdy, rides the ferry a lot.
He also falls for an island girl.
Her name is (drumroll, please!)
Nina.

So where would the novel
go from here? Adam and Zoey
ride off into the sunset while
Nina and Julius do calculus prob-

lems and take square-dancing lessons?

Oh, the unfairness of it all!
And to think that this is the
story of my _life._

But then again, what does
it really matter whether it's
Adam or Julius who falls in
love with me....when the only
one I want is Benjamin, anyway?

Fifteen

"That's it," Nina said, closing the book. "I'm going on strike."

"What?" Benjamin said from the bed, where he lay in darkness. "Why?"

"Because you keep making me read these awful books," Nina said. "First *The Exorcist* and now *Misery*. I was scared to death."

"No kidding," Benjamin said. "Your voice was shaking all over the place."

"Well, can you blame me?" Nina asked. "I had nightmares, too. I kept seeing Claire floating down the hall toward me with her tongue flicking in and out."

Benjamin frowned. "Claire?"

"Yes, she seemed a natural in the role," Nina said. She sounded thoughtful. "I wonder if she *is* possessed. That would explain, like, eighteen years of behavior."

"Nina—"

"I'm going to ask her if her bed has ever levitated," Nina said. "Anyway, I'm officially on strike, so now I'm going to read you questions from my driving test and you're going to help me study."

"Okay," Benjamin said agreeably.

He heard Nina rustling around in her backpack and the sound of a book opening. "All right," she said, reading. "You are traveling on a fast road in good conditions. How can you be sure you are following at a safe distance?"

Benjamin started to answer, but she cut him off. "Wait a minute; it's multiple choice. *(a)* There should be a two-second time gap between you and the car in front of you. *(b)* The distance between you and the car in front should be your braking distance. *(c)* The distance between you and the car in front should be twice the length of your vehicle."

"*C,*" Benjamin said.

"You think so?" Nina asked. "I was going to guess the one about the two-second gap."

"Two seconds?" Benjamin said. "No wonder you keep rear-ending people."

"Well, let me look up the answer," Nina said, and he heard pages turning. "Hey, you're right."

"You have to picture the cars," Benjamin said. "Try it; it's easy."

"I'm trying," Nina said. "Which car am I driving?"

"Nina . . ."

"Oh, I give up!" Nina said. "This is just like old times!"

Benjamin's watch beeped, signaling that his four hours were over. He sat up and stripped off his mask. "What's just like old times?" he asked.

"You doing better on tests just by visualizing it," Nina said. "Just like you did when you were blind."

Benjamin looked at her. "Did you like the 'old times'?"

She hesitated, then nodded. "Did you?"

Benjamin started to shake his head and then considered. "Not everything about them," he said. "But some things, yes. Some things I liked very much."

And they smiled at each other in the dim light.

Zoey felt dishonest as she carried the plate of hash browns up to the construction site.

I'm not doing anything wrong, she argued with herself. *I'm just asking Lucas for a favor . . . and bringing him a bribe.*

"Hi, Lucas," she said, and her voice sounded unnaturally bright to her own ears.

"Hi," Lucas said. He glanced up at her, but he didn't stop sanding the floorboard he was working on, and Zoey realized with embarrassment that she had expected him to.

So he's not hanging on my every word, she thought. *Fine. I can live without that.*

"I brought you some hash browns," she said.

"Oh, okay," Lucas said, and his voice was cold. She had a momentary fear that he would tell her to leave the plate, but to her relief, he put down the electric sander and stood up. "Thanks," he said. "I'm hungry."

Zoey handed him the plate and then lingered, balancing casually on one foot. "Actually," she said, "I wanted to ask you a favor."

Lucas had his mouth full, but he raised his eyebrows. Zoey didn't care for that look at all. *Go ahead,* it seemed to say. *Let's hear it.*

"Well," she said, swallowing. "I have to write this thing for the Historical Society, and one of the people I'm supposed to interview won't talk to me unless I take him out to the actual site of the shipwreck."

"What shipwreck?" Lucas asked.

"The *Carolina*?" she said.

He nodded, and Zoey waited for him to say something, but he didn't.

"Anyway," she said. "I, um, really need to talk to this man, and I was wondering, well, hoping that you would take him and me out in your dad's fishing boat."

"It's my fishing boat," Lucas said, standing up and holding the empty plate out to her. "That's what I do now. I'm a fisherman."

Why is he being *like this?* Zoey wondered. "Okay," she said, trying to keep her voice gentle. "Your fishing boat, then."

Lucas looked at her, and his eyes were flat. "Why don't you get Adam to do it?" he asked, and there was just enough emphasis on the word *Adam* for Zoey to realize that Lucas knew about the kiss. She didn't know how he'd found out, but he knew. "I'm sure he'd be happy to do it, seeing as how he's your *cousin* and all."

For a moment, Zoey was stunned. *Well, fine,* she thought. *I'm not his girlfriend anymore. I can kiss whomever I want.*

She kept her voice level. "Adam is my *second* cousin *and* he's adopted. Besides, he doesn't have a fishing boat."

Lucas bit his lip. "You'd have to reimburse me for the gas," he said finally.

"Sure," Zoey said, and without thinking she stuck out her hand and they shook on it, like businessmen, or diplomats, or strangers.

124

Sixteen

Aisha did go to the library but not to study. She found an empty carrel in the imposing splendor of Cabot Science Library and dumped her books on it. The she rummaged through her backpack and took out the flowered notebook she had taken from Felicia's drawer an hour earlier: Felicia's diary.

Aisha pushed her textbooks to the far corner of her desktop, looked around guiltily, and then carefully opened the diary.

August 19

God, I hate it here.

Aisha blinked. She wasn't sure quite what she had expected to find in Felicia's diary, but that bitter first sentence shocked her. She read on.

August 19
God, I hate it here. I hate everything about Harvard, just like I knew I would. Why wouldn't Mommy and Daddy let me go to Berkeley? I know I could be happy there, and not just because of Marcus. Why do I have to go to Harvard just because Daddy did? Who

wants to go to college in the same boring town where they went to high school with the same boring bunch of creeps? Why, oh, why did I study so hard? If I'd gotten worse grades or worse SATs, then I couldn't have come here.

Aisha closed the diary and sat at her desk, open-mouthed. Felicia was *from* Cambridge? She had told Aisha she was from New York! And all the friends that Felicia seemed to make so easily and quickly—they were high school pals? It was unbelievable. And who was Marcus? Aisha opened the diary again, and her eyes sped hungrily across the page.

August 20

More "great" news. I'm going to have a roommate. Damn. I applied for a single, but they say they have to put this girl somewhere because of some screwup in administration. Lucky me. Her name is Aisha Gray. Aisha and Felicia. That sounds so cutesy, I could throw up.

Well, I can't help my name, Aisha thought. Then another thought occurred to her. Felicia had never wanted a roommate at all. So all the fantasies Aisha had nurtured, fantasies of a roommate who would be her new best friend, were doomed to failure before she even started.

August 21

Marcus still hasn't called, and he promised to call every day! I can't believe he only left for Berkeley three days ago. It seems like three years. Well, maybe our number's not listed. I'm sure if he called Mommy and Daddy, they wouldn't give it to him.

Aisha paused, chewing the inside of her cheek thoughtfully. Marcus must be the boy in the picture she'd found in Felicia's desk. The handsome boy with the deep tan and the reckless smile. So Marcus had gone to Berkeley, and Felicia had wanted to go there with him, but her parents hadn't approved. Why? Aisha wondered. Did they think Marcus and Felicia were getting too serious?

August 22
Well, I called campus information, and my phone number is definitely listed. I guess I should say our phone number because my roommate arrived—complete with tiny silver diamond engagement ring and pictures of her hometown sweetheart. It's all so provincial, I can't believe it. Just what I need.

Hey, I just thought of something. What if Marcus doesn't have a phone? He could call me from a pay phone, of course, but he probably wants to talk to me in private.

August 29
Still no word from Marcus. I can't understand it. Of course, our phone rings off the hook, but it's always that stupid Christopher for Aisha.

But that's not true! Aisha thought. *The phone rings all the time for Felicia. I always felt like such a loser—but—but I guess she did, too.*

Today I went home for Sunday dinner, and during the cocktail hour Daddy asked me very pointedly how Marcus was. I looked him in the eye and said, "Fine. We talk every day. Marcus had to get a part-time job just to pay for the phone bills." Daddy looked away.

But I hated Marcus for making me lie. Why isn't he calling? He promised. He promised to love me forever!

I wonder when he promised you that? Aisha thought. *Was it right before you slept with him? It sounds like Mommy and Daddy were right to disapprove of him.*

September 1

I broke down and called Marcus's parents. His mother answered, and I said, "Hello, Mrs. Thompson, this is Felicia," and she said, "Yes?" and I said, "Felicia Sherritt," and she said, "Yes, how can I help you, dear?" and I was quiet for a long minute, and then I said I was a friend of Marcus's from high school and I wondered if she had his new number, and she said, "Oh, of course, let me go get it."

I couldn't believe it. I was so sure she would say, "Oh, dear, haven't you heard? Marcus is—" Marcus is what? In traction? I guess I didn't have a very clear idea of what she was going to tell me. But I hung up before she got back because I could tell by her voice that she had no idea who I was even though Marcus said once that after the first time we met on the beach, he went home and told his mother that he'd found the perfect girl, the only girl in the world for him.

> *September 3*
> *I want to change our phone number so that Marcus can't call me, but I don't have the nerve. Because what if he calls after all this time with a perfectly reasonable explanation?*

But he never did, Aisha realized with a wave of reluctant sympathy. *Oh, Felicia, he never called. I know because Marcus is an unusual name and I would have remembered it. Oh, my God, you've been waiting for him to call for months, and he hasn't. Is this why you don't date anyone?*

> *September 4*
> *Some girl called for Aisha tonight, and when she left her number, I recognized the Berkeley area code right away, so I tried to draw her into conversation. It wasn't hard. Her name is Zoey, and she's from the same little nothing town in Maine, and she and Aisha have been friends since junior high, yawn, yawn. So after some long incredibly boring conversation I asked her if she knew Marcus, but she didn't.*

So that's why she was interested in Zoey! Aisha thought. *I thought she liked her, but she just wanted a spy.*

> *September 10*
> *God, if I have to listen to one more phone conversation between Aisha and Christopher, I'm going to kill myself. "I love you." "Not as*

much as I love you." "No, I love you twice as much as you love me." Etc., etc. Jesus, and this is a girl who has a scholarship.

Aisha cringed, remembering that conversation. *Why didn't I have the sense to wait until I was alone to talk like that? Would I want to hear Felicia talk to someone like that? Especially if I were waiting for Christopher to call me for months and months?*
She flipped through the pages.

Aisha says she's so sure of Christopher. . . . Aisha says she and Christopher have been through a lot and he would never betray her. . . . Aisha says Christopher is perfect for her. . . . Aisha says she's never looked at another man. . . . Aisha says . . . Aisha says . . .

Did I really say all those things? Aisha wondered. *Why? What was the point? To prove to Felicia how lucky I was? I must have sounded so cruel, but I didn't know about Marcus! How could I? If only she'd told me!*
She kept reading.

September 12
God, I have so much work to do. Three exams in one week. I think I'm going to have a nervous breakdown. I was so desperate, I even tried to call Aisha's boyfriend because she said he was some sort of history buff. All I got was his answering machine. Not that he would have been much help, anyway. I'm sure he's just as countrified as she is.

130

Aisha blinked. *She thinks he's countrified!* she thought. *Who would have thought it would make me happy to hear someone insult him? But she really was calling him for help. Oh, and I was so sure she was calling him to—to—*

She couldn't even remember why she thought Felicia had called anymore. Her brain was reeling with all the new information. She began turning the pages more rapidly.

Felicia had obtained Marcus's number from the Berkeley student directory and was pranking him regularly despite some caller ID fears. She also had a crush on one of her professors, although she wasn't sure if he already had a girlfriend. *Gosh, that would never occur to me,* Aisha thought. *I would just assume he wouldn't go out with a student.*

She flipped ahead until she found the entry she was looking for.

> *October 13*
> *Aisha told me that her boyfriend was coming to visit, and I was like, oh, fantastic, a weekend in Saccharin City, but then Christopher got here and he looks so much like Marcus, I couldn't believe it. I never noticed the resemblance in her pictures.*

Christopher doesn't look like Marcus, Aisha thought indignantly. But even as she thought it, she wondered if it might be true. She thought back to the picture she'd seen in Felicia's desk. Maybe . . .

> *Christopher invited me along to the museum, and Aisha practically went up in*

smoke. I probably shouldn't have gone, but I couldn't resist. Girls who are too insecure to deal with another girl's presence don't deserve boyfriends.

Anyway, I spent the day with them, and Aisha was really witchy and made it clear that she wished a fiery pit would open up and swallow me. God, I hate girls like that! Girls who are all buddy-buddy until there's a man around.

But I'm not usually like that! Aisha thought. *I hate girls like that, too. And I was never buddy-buddy with Felicia before Christopher was around, either.*

I had planned to be wearing this baby doll nightgown and sort of be puttering around the room when Aisha and Christopher got home last night, but they were so late that eventually I got into bed. I still had the nightgown on, but I had the covers pulled up, so they didn't get the full view, so to speak.

Christopher saw enough to make his eyes bug out a little bit, but then he didn't meet my eyes or smile or anything. I'm kind of sorry I did it because Christopher basically treated me like a billboard or something, like I was just something to look at but not to get involved with. It's unfathomable, but he's definitely devoted to Minnie Mouse.

Aisha closed the book and held it to her chest. **Yes,** she thought, *yes, he is totally devoted to Minnie Mouse.*

Suddenly she didn't want to read any more. She just wanted to hurry back to their room and put Felicia's diary back before she noticed it was missing.

But when Aisha got there, Felicia was gone, and she didn't come home all night.

Claire

Some things are so disgusting that you don't even want to write them in your diary. But then again, you certainly don't want to <u>tell</u> anyone about it, either. And I guess my diary can bring itself to hear about, how I threw up in the O'Connells' sink.

But I keep thinking about this time when we were really little, and my mother was still alive, and the whole family was driving someplace. Anyway, Nina leaned forward and said, "Dad, I don't feel so good." Dad said, "What kind of bad do you feel?" and Nina said, "Carsick," and then she threw up into the front seat. And even though my parents were really sweet about it, you could tell that they wished she'd given them like two more seconds' warning so they could've pulled over.

And once at homecoming the homecoming queen, Kitty Crawford, and her date went out for dinner and had raw oysters. Only it turned out that Kitty was allergic to oysters, and she threw up right onstage and splashed her dress, and even though everyone was really nice to her, it was amazingly gross.

So what do you think it was like for Paolo's family, who didn't even like me to begin with?

135

Seventeen

The sound of Mr. Samuels's pen seemed very loud to Nina as he graded her final exam.

"How'd I do?" she asked, nervously shredding a Lucky Strike. The desktop in front of her was covered with tobacco fragments. "Did I pass?"

Mr. Samuels sighed and made a last mark. "You passed," he said briefly.

"I did?" Nina asked. "I *did?*" She jumped to her feet, spraying tobacco everywhere. "I passed! Oh, Benjamin, did you hear that? I passed!"

"I heard," Benjamin said mildly from the back of the room, where he was playing with Mr. Samuels's collection of Matchbox cars.

Nina crossed her arms and cupped her elbows, hugging herself. "Oh, I knew it! I knew I was right about that question asking which way to point the wheels when you're parking on a hill! I knew—"

"Actually you got that one wrong," Mr. Samuels said.

Nina dropped her arms. "I did?"

Mr. Samuels nodded.

"Well, how many did I get right?" Nina asked.

Mr. Samuels glanced at her paper. "Seven."

"Seven?" Benjamin said from the back. "Seven out of twenty?"

"Oh, be quiet," Nina said. "Seven's passing, isn't it?"

"Actually it's not," Mr. Samuels said.

"But you said I passed!" Nina protested.

"Yes, I did," Mr. Samuels said. "You passed because I didn't want to deal with you anymore. You or your friend Zoey."

"She's not my friend," Nina said instantly. "And don't tell me *she* passed."

"She got seven out of twenty, just like you," Mr. Samuels said implacably. "And I passed her, just like I'm passing you."

"You've got to be kidding!" Nina said, her voice trembling with indignation. "Zoey Passmore is a menace to society! She's a danger to herself and others! I can't believe you passed her. I—I ought to report you to the Food and Drug Administration."

"The Food and Drug Administration?" Mr. Samuels looked confused. "What do they have to do with anything?"

"Because you must *be* on drugs to pass Zoey!" Nina said, completely carried away. "Anybody could see that she can't drive her way out of a paper bag and you—Benjamin, let go!"

Benjamin's hand had closed over her arm with a grip like iron. "Thank you, sir," he said to Mr. Samuels. "We have to be going."

"We don't have to be going!" Nina said. "I'm just getting started—I—hey—"

But Benjamin propelled her out into the hall.

She shook off his arm. "Why did you do that?"

"Because I thought he might change his mind,"

Benjamin said. He shook his head. "Seven out of twenty! Nina, really."

Nina made a face. "Look, that test was loaded with trick questions. You ought to try taking it."

"I did take it," Benjamin pointed out, holding the door open for her. "Anyone who has a driver's license has taken that test. You must have passed it once before yourself. I have no idea *how,* but you must have."

"So what are you saying?" Nina asked as they crossed the parking lot. "That the entire population is made up of people who are smarter than me?"

"I didn't say that," Benjamin said. "You did."

"Oh, very funny," Nina said.

They got in her car and shut the doors. "I still can't believe he passed Zoey," she said, putting the car in gear and driving across the lot. "You should have seen her during that braking exercise. It was like being in a car driven by a kangaroo."

"A kangaroo?" Benjamin asked.

"Well, some jumpy hyper animal," Nina said. "Aren't kangaroos hyper? Anyway—"

"Hey, will you look where you're going?" Benjamin interrupted.

"I'm looking, I'm looking," Nina said. "Why does everyone always say that to me?"

"Because you always look at the person you're talking to," Benjamin said. "And it's unnerving."

"It's not unnerving," Nina said. "It's plain good manners. I hate it when the driver doesn't look at me."

"Yes, well, it's just that I have this desire to get back to North Harbor alive," Benjamin said.

"Oh, so now I'm endangering your life?" Nina said. "Listen, I'm making a new rule, effective immediately: Passengers in this car cannot criticize my

138

driving. If you don't have anything nice to say, don't say anything. Especially about tailgating, because if there's anything I can't stand, it's backseat drivers telling me I'm following too closely and—"

The sound of the collision cut her off.

Nina closed her eyes and leaned her head against the steering wheel.

"My dad is going to kill me," she moaned.

"Not if Zoey gets to you first," Benjamin said.

Nina opened her eyes. "What does Zoey have to do with anything?"

"She's driving the car in front of us," Benjamin said.

Claire sat at the antique desk in the living room, freshly showered, wearing sweats and Reebok cross trainers. Janelle had made waffles to soothe her hangover. Burke was making phone calls in the kitchen, and his deep voice soothed her homesickness. Soon Nina would be home from traffic school, and she would make Claire laugh and that would soothe her melancholy mood. Yes, Claire was feeling much better.

She just had one unpleasant chore to do. She was drafting a letter on a yellow legal pad.

Dear Mr. and Mrs. O'Connell,

That was as far as she had gotten. Now she picked up the pencil again.

Dear Mr. and Mrs. O'Connell,
  Thank you so much for the lovely

*weekend in Princeton. I can't tell you
what a pleasure it was to meet you
both. Paolo has spoken of you often.*

Claire paused briefly and counted the number of
lies in her first three sentences. Three: The weekend
wasn't lovely, it wasn't pleasurable to meet them,
and Paolo hadn't talked about them very much.
Three lies in under thirty words seemed a little
extreme, so she tore off that piece of paper and
started over.

*Dear Mr. and Mrs. O'Connell,
    Thank you so much for letting me
stay with you Friday and Saturday
night. I'm sorry I had to leave so
abruptly this morning, but something
came up.*

My dinner came up, Claire thought. *In their sink
last night. I better not write that.*
She crossed out the second sentence and wrote:

*I'm sorry for leaving without
saying good-bye, but I wasn't feeling
too well.*

140

This is impossible! she thought. *Obviously I wasn't feeling well—I thought my head was going to fall off my shoulders and smash like a pumpkin. They're bound to know how hung over I was.*

She picked up the pencil and wrote with determination:

Dear Mr. and Mrs. O'Connell,

Thank you so much for letting me stay with you Friday and Saturday night. You seem like really nice people. Please give my regards to Fathers Miguel and Brendan. I'm sorry I left without saying good-bye.

Yours,
Claire Geiger

There. No lies. She was recopying the note onto a piece of stationery when the doorbell rang.

"I'll get it," Burke called.

Claire heard his footsteps in the foyer and the sound of the door opening. "Hello?" Burke said.

"Hello, Mr. Geiger!" cried a joyous voice.

It was Paolo.

Eighteen

Because the van was so big, Zoey didn't even see the car that had rear-ended her until she climbed out of the driver's side and walked back to behold Nina emerging from her father's Mercedes.

"Oh, well, this figures," Zoey said sarcastically, putting her hands on her hips. "This just figures—" She broke off as Benjamin opened the passenger door and stepped out. "Benjamin! Are you all right?"

He nodded. "I'm fine."

"What about me?" Nina said. "Don't you care if I'm all right? I could have whiplash."

Zoey turned back to her. "Why would you have whiplash when you're the one who rear-ended *me?* I can't believe you caused an accident on the same day you finished driving school."

Nina's brows drew together. "I didn't cause this! You did!"

"Oh, spare me," Zoey said heatedly. "I was just an innocent bystander."

"Innocent bystanders don't drive down main roads at ten miles an hour," Nina shot back. "That's just begging for trouble."

"I was looking for my turn," Zoey protested.

"Then why didn't you have your turn signal on?" Nina asked.

"You wouldn't know if I had my turn signal on or not," Zoey said fervently, ignoring the fact that they had caused a traffic jam and passing drivers were staring at them. "Because I bet you anything you were talking to Benjamin and had your head turned completely sideways!"

"That's not the issue!" Nina shouted, holding a finger up in the air. "The question is, *Did you have your turn signal on?* and—Benjamin, will you stop laughing?"

"I can't help it," Benjamin said, sitting on the crumpled fender of the Mercedes and shaking his head. "It's too hilarious. What are the odds of you two getting in an accident—"

"What are you, a statistician?" Nina asked, annoyed.

"And it's not funny," Zoey snapped. "Look at the back of our van!"

"Well, look at the front of my car!" Nina yelled. "Why are you acting like this is so much worse for you?"

"Because it *is!*" Zoey yelled back. "Because my dad and Benjamin and I are trying to run a restaurant and get back on our feet, and the last thing we need is a big car-repair bill."

"Oh, don't give me that," Nina snapped. "Insurance will cover it."

"What if it doesn't?" Zoey asked. "What if—if your insurance company drops you?" She had no idea if such a thing was possible, but she was happy to see a little dart of fear cross Nina's face.

"That's not going to happen," Nina said uncertainly.

"Well, even if it doesn't, it will still mean that I'll have to deal with you and your father," Zoey said, shouting to be heard above the noise of some idiot honking at them.

Nina's expression turned to anger more quickly than Zoey would have thought possible. "Oh, that's it, isn't it?" she said, advancing on Zoey. "You might have to deal with me, or talk to me, or acknowledge my existence, and that would really *inconvenience* you, wouldn't it?"

"That's—," Zoey started, but Nina wouldn't let her finish. She took another step toward Zoey.

"Well, I'm so sorry," Nina said, "that I haven't shriveled up and ceased to exist just because you don't like me anymore. I'm so sorry that despite having lost my status as your friend, I've had the audaciousness—"

"Audacity," Benjamin supplied.

"Yes, the audacity to go on living," Nina said. "I suppose at the very least I should have joined a convent and repented for the rest of my life. Well, I'm sorry, Zoey. I'm sorry that I continue to selfishly hang around and make your life miserable. I'm sorry that you have to see me on the street, I'm sorry that I hit your car today, I'm sorry about Lucas, I'm sorry I lied to you, I'm sorry I wasn't a better friend, I'm sorry you wouldn't let me apologize to you, I'm sorry that I keep on missing you even though you hate me, and I'm sorry—*I'm just so sorry!*"

And suddenly Nina buried her face in her hands, and even over the traffic Zoey could make out the sounds of her crying.

Zoey stared at her in amazement. Nina . . . missed her? How could Nina miss her?

Nina gave an especially loud sob, and Zoey

stepped forward and put her arms around her. "Shhh," she said softly as Nina's arms went around her neck in a strangling grip. "It's okay, Nina. I miss you, too, and now it's going to be okay. All right? All right?"

But Nina only pressed her wet cheek against Zoey's shoulder and nodded while Zoey patted her back and murmured to her in the same way she had soothed her about dropped ice-cream cones and broken dolls when they were much, much younger.

Claire hurried into the front hall to find Paolo shaking Burke's hand enthusiastically. Burke looked so awkward and yet so absurdly pleased that Claire laughed out loud.

Paolo and Burke turned toward her, and Paolo's look was so cold that the laughter stuck in Claire's throat. She coughed slightly and said, "Dad, this is Paolo O'Connell."

"Yes, we've met," Burke said wryly. "How do you do?"

"I'm all right," Paolo said, his eyes never leaving Claire.

She smiled at him, but he didn't smile back.

He's mad at me, she realized.

The thought made her heart beat rapidly. She didn't know why, but she suddenly couldn't bear the thought of Paolo being mad at her. Which didn't make sense because *she'd* been mad at *him* practically from the first day they'd met, but she couldn't help it. Paolo being mad at her made her feel horrible.

"Do you want to come into the living room?" she asked shyly.

Paolo nodded.

"I'm going to run to the store," Burke said suddenly. "Nice to meet you, Paolo."

"You too, Mr. Geiger," Paolo said, smiling.

Oh, fine, Claire thought. *Be nice to* him.

She led the way into the living room and gestured for Paolo to take a seat. She was disappointed when he sat in an armchair. Now there was no way she could sit next to him. She sat in a matching chair, curling her legs under her.

"This is a surprise," she said warmly.

Paolo shrugged and sat forward. He picked a piece of rock candy out of a dish on the coffee table and popped it in his mouth.

"Don't eat that," Claire said. "Nina made it in home ec about five years ago."

She hoped he would smile, but he didn't, although he did spit the piece of candy into an ashtray. Then he sat back and looked at her.

"Well, I don't have to ask where you went," he said, "because I guessed right and found you here. So now the only question is why you left without even telling me."

"Oh, Paolo," Claire said, leaning forward. "I'm sorry. I was just so embarrassed."

"You were embarrassed?" Paolo asked bitterly. "How do you think it feels to be stood up by your girlfriend in front of your entire family?"

Claire bit her lip. *He just called me his girlfriend,* she thought. *His parents and his sisters called me that, but not Paolo.*

"I'm sorry if I embarrassed you," she said, struggling to keep her voice even. "But I just couldn't face everyone—"

"That's crap," Paolo said.

Claire was startled. "What?"

"That's crap," he said again. "You never get embarrassed."

"Paolo," she protested. "Didn't enough things happen this weekend to embarrass anyone? Didn't I drop the condom and throw up and—"

"Yes," Paolo said shortly. "But I know you, and you don't get embarrassed. Not by anything. So tell me why you left."

"I did tell you," Claire said angrily, getting up and walking away from him. She sat in the window seat. "I did tell you, but you've decided that embarrassment is not an emotion I'm capable of. What else can I do?"

Paolo watched her. "You don't care what people think of you," he said. "Why should my family be any different?"

"Because they are!" Claire burst out. "Because I wanted them to like me. I wanted them to like me so much, I was afraid of opening my mouth! And it went wrong, completely wrong, and you know it!" Her voice wavered. "You're right about me never caring about what people think of me, but this time I did! *This time I did!*"

"Shhh," Paolo said, crossing to her quickly. "Shhh, Clara, it's all right." He tried to hold her hands, but she shook him off and stood up.

"It's not all right!" she yelled. "It's horrible. I don't like feeling this way!"

"What way is that?" Paolo asked, taking her hands again and pulling her back down onto the window seat. He knelt in front of her. "Feeling what way? That you care? That you care about me so much that you were nervous around my family?"

Claire wiped the back of her hand across her nose. *"Yes."*

147

Paolo smiled slowly. "Is that really so horrible?" he asked softly.

Claire looked at him for a long moment, and then she too smiled. "I guess not," she said.

The warmth had come back into Paolo's eyes, and his hand tightened on hers. Claire leaned forward and kissed him. Paolo was shaking.

They both were.

Zoey

Things were going well with Lucas, and now they're not. Things were going badly with Nina, and now they're not.

I don't get it. Why can't everything go well with everyone all at once? Don't get me wrong; I am incredibly glad to have made up with Nina. In fact, now that we're talking again, we have so much to say that sometimes I'm afraid I'll never have time to do anything else again.

Actually, that doesn't sound so bad to me.

But still....I can't help feeling like it's only part of the puzzle. Like there's something missing.

I am so lucky to have met Adam. I mean, he's really sweet and handsome...and kissing him was incredible.

But...what?

I don't know. I just don't know.

Nineteen

The old codger that Zoey was interviewing took one look at Lucas's fishing boat and announced, "This is an exceptionally small vessel."

"Well, yes," Lucas said. "That's why it's a fishing boat and not a cruise ship. Go ahead."

The old codger held up one finger. "Ladies first."

Lucas sighed. "Zoey?"

"Right here," she said from behind him. She was checking the batteries on her tape recorder. "Excuse me, Mr. Ruggles," she said, and climbed onto the boat.

Mr. Ruggles followed her, and Lucas went last, casting off the lines.

Zoey and Mr. Ruggles were already in the cabin.

"I'm steering," Mr. Ruggles announced.

"No way," Lucas said.

"But she promised!" Mr. Ruggles said, pointing at Zoey.

"Mr. Ruggles!" Zoey exclaimed sternly. "I did no such thing. Now come over and sit by me on this bench."

Mr. Ruggles sat next to Zoey and looked around the cabin critically while Lucas started the boat and steered them out of the marina. Then he looked at Zoey. "You have exquisite hips, miss," he said.

Zoey shook her head.

"Where did you find this guy?" Lucas asked.

"In the phone book," Mr. Ruggles answered promptly. "And if I don't get to steer for at least five minutes, I'm not going to tell her anything."

Lucas rolled his eyes. "Oh, all right," he said, since they were out of the marina, anyway. "You know where we're going?"

"I couldn't forget those coordinates in a hundred years," Mr. Ruggles said, and Lucas supposed this was true enough.

He handed over the wheel and then took the seat next to Zoey, who smiled at him wryly.

"Sorry," she whispered.

"It's okay," Lucas said.

She dug around in her backpack. "How much do I owe you for gas?"

Lucas was tempted to say, *How about another fried-egg sandwich?* but he didn't want to force Zoey to visit him if she didn't want to. Not after seeing her with Adam.

"Five dollars should cover it," he said finally.

She handed him the money. "Thank you so much," she said, whispering again. "I know Mr. Ruggles is a handful, but without him I wouldn't have a hope of finishing this piece."

Lucas thought she looked as though she'd been working hard. She wore no makeup, and a baseball cap was jammed on her head backward. Lucas knew she did that when her hair was dirty.

"It's okay," he said.

"We're there," Mr. Ruggles announced, cutting the engine.

"Already?" Zoey asked. "This close to shore?"

"It only took the rescue ship seven minutes to reach us," Mr. Ruggles said gravely, "and in that time thirty-two men died in the subzero water."

"*Wait!*" Zoey screamed. "I need to get that on tape!"

But Mr. Ruggles had already stumped out of the cabin and was on deck, looking out over the starry water.

"It started early that morning," he said as Zoey and Lucas caught up with him. "I woke up when I felt the rhythm of the ship change, and ten minutes later it was clear that we'd taken on water. The ship was limping."

"What had happened?" Lucas asked.

"Don't know," Mr. Ruggles said thoughtfully. "Could have been an iceberg, could have been a whale."

"Were you scared?" Zoey asked.

"Not at first, no," Mr. Ruggles said. "The captain said that we were going to make for the first available harbor, which was Chatham Island, fifty miles away. He told us that another ship, the *Brandywine,* was forty miles behind us, but she had us on her radar, and she would tail us until we got to shelter.

"At noon the captain said that there wouldn't be any lunch, that he needed all hands on deck, and I began to feel a little nervous then. About four o'clock in the afternoon I asked him how far we'd come, and he said about twenty-five miles, and right then I began praying.

"I never worked so hard in my life to keep a ship going. We all did. And nobody said a word. Didn't have to because we were all thinking the same thing, anyway. Then about nine o'clock the captain announced we were only twenty miles from North Harbor, and a huge cheer went up. But the captain didn't cheer, I remember noticing that.

"At ten the *Brandywine* radioed in and asked how we were doing, and the captain radioed back that Chatham Island was waiting for us, that they were standing by with lifeboats. The last thing he said was, 'We are holding our own.'"

Mr. Ruggles was silent for a long time. "Something gave way belowdecks about ten minutes after that," he said. "You could just feel it, like a big whoosh, and right away the stern began tilting. I never saw a ship sink so fast in my life.

"We could see the lights of the rescue ship coming toward us even as the first waves broke over the prow and we felt how cold the water was."

Mr. Ruggles took a deep breath. "Before that night I always said I wanted to die quickly in an accident, car or boat, didn't matter to me. I just didn't want to linger for weeks with some sickness."

Mr. Ruggles scratched his chin. "Well, I can tell you now that I'll take an illness any day because when you think you're about to die, you realize that there's a lot of things you want to put right, and a lot of folks you ought to forgive for old wrongs, and a lot of folks you want to tell you're sorry and that you love them, and there's just no more time."

Lucas looked out over the starry, smooth water and tried not to imagine that night, the men sliding one by one into the frigid water, their brief screams, the quiet, the waiting.

Then he realized something with a start.

Zoey was staring at him.

* * *

Zoey was trembling, big violent spasms that shook her whole body and made her teeth chatter.

Mr. Ruggles's words echoed in her brain . . . *You realize that there's a lot of things you want to put right . . . a lot of folks you ought to forgive for old wrongs . . . and tell them that you love them, and there's just no more time. . . .*

Zoey thought about her ferry ride with Adam last night and how magical it had seemed, but how it was now tarnishing in front of her eyes. Because if she were dying, would she think of Adam?

She closed her eyes. No, she would think of Lucas and this smelly fishing boat and her unwashed hair and how none of it mattered, none of it mattered in the slightest; the only thing that mattered, the only thing that she had ever cared about, that had ever made her happy—

"Oh, Lucas!" she wailed, and threw herself into his arms.

She closed her eyes and soaked up the smell and feel of Lucas. His arms went around her and held her tight, and Zoey knew suddenly that she would never have to explain this moment to Lucas. He would understand.

I can hear my heart beating, she thought suddenly, but it was only the low-battery warning on her tape recorder.

"Kissing," Mr. Ruggles said in disgust. "It figures."

155

Twenty

Aisha was getting off the bus in front of her dorm when she noticed that her resident adviser, Sherry, was getting on.

"Sherry," she said quickly, laying her hand on Sherry's arm. "Have you seen Felicia?"

"Sure," Sherry said. "She's taking a shower."

"Right now?" Aisha asked.

Sherry nodded. "She was headed into the bathroom just as I was coming out. About two seconds ago."

"Oh, okay, thanks," Aisha said uncertainly.

Sherry smiled. "Why? Did she stay out all night without calling? Oh, sorry, the bus is going to leave. Bye!"

"Bye," Aisha said, happy that she didn't have to explain that she and Felicia weren't the kind of roommates who would dream of calling each other to say they were staying out all night. Only friends did that.

Aisha walked slowly into the dorm, pausing in the lobby to pick up her mail.

So Felicia was home and not dead on the street somewhere. She had been gone for almost twenty-four hours. But where had she gone, and why? Had she noticed that her diary had gone AWOL for a few hours?

Well, if she did notice, she'll tell me, Aisha thought. *That's one thing about Felicia; she doesn't hold anything back.*

She got onto the elevator and pressed her floor number.

What would she say if Felicia confronted her? *I'm so sorry, Felicia, but I was feeling nervous and insecure, and I hope you don't mind. . . .*

That would never work. *If she had read my diary, I would have nothing but contempt for her,* Aisha thought. *I have some contempt for myself right now, too, but that didn't stop me from doing what I did. But I'm not sorry.*

The elevator doors opened, and she stepped out onto her floor.

Well, if Felicia accused her of reading her diary, Aisha would admit it and then accuse Felicia of a few things herself, like trying to seduce Christopher.

She took a deep breath and opened the door to their room.

Felicia was talking on the telephone, her back to the door. She was wearing a beautiful gold-and-black matching bra-and-panty set.

Felicia giggled into the phone, her fingertips touching the black lace at the edge of her bra. "Well, did you ever see that Madonna video with the bullfighter? It's the same one she wore. . . . Gold with a black filigree pattern . . . Filigree means lacy. . . ."

So much for roommate confrontations, Aisha thought. *It's like living with a calendar pinup or something.*

"What else can I tell you?" Felicia said into the phone. "It's just basic underwear." She giggled again.

Basic, my ass, Aisha realized. *Basic underwear is white cotton and elastic.*

She threw her backpack onto her bed noisily, signaling her arrival.

Felicia turned, hesitated, and then gave her a kind of baby wave. She seemed about to say something else into the phone, but then she changed her mind and held the phone out to Aisha.

"It's for you," she said, again with that hesitation. "It's Christopher."

Aisha's hand was filled with helium. It was that simple. One moment she was reaching for the phone, and now her hand just hung in the air, hovering slightly, and she was powerless to move it up or down.

Christopher was on the phone? Her Christopher? Was he the only Christopher they knew? Yes. But . . . had he really been asking Felicia to describe her underwear? Had he—

She looked up suddenly and saw the exhilarated look in Felicia's eyes for a full second before Felicia could look away.

This is a test, Aisha thought. *She wants to see if I meant everything I said about loving Christopher. She wants to know if I'm too insecure to handle the "competition."*

Aisha lifted her chin and took the phone. "Nice outfit," she said to Felicia. She put the phone to her ear. "Christopher?"

She listened for a moment.

"I love you, too," Aisha said, and passed the test.

Twenty-one

8:01 A.M.

Zoey begins first draft of the dedication speech.

8:13 A.M.

Nina calls Zoey to get in an extra few minutes of conversation before school.

9:03 A.M.

Lucas calls Zoey to tell her that he loves her. Unfortunately he does it on a cellular phone, which means that he's telling all the fishermen in a thirty-mile radius that he loves them, too.

9:04 A.M.

Aisha calls Christopher to tell him that she loves him. He asks her to come home, and she's says it isn't possible; she has a big test on Wednesday.

9:10 A.M.

Paolo is served Janelle's waffles and invited to stay for dinner. He accepts.

9:12 A.M.

Aisha decides that if she studies without stopping on the entire bus trip to and from North Harbor, she'll do fine on her test. Well, she'll do okay on her test.

10:01 A.M.

Zoey begins second draft of dedication speech.

10:02 A.M.

Aisha boards Maine-bound bus.

12:01 P.M.

Zoey begins third draft of dedication speech.

1:34 P.M.

Lucas calls Zoey to tell her that he loves her and that fishermen have been whistling at him all day.

2:05 P.M.

Julius McMartin gives Nina a corsage.

3:01 P.M.

Zoey begins fourth draft of dedication speech.

3:15 P.M.

Nina goes over to see Zoey at the Grays' and starts talking.

4:08 P.M.

Aisha stares out the bus window, her chemistry book open on her lap.

5:24 P.M.

Nina pauses for breath.

5:25 P.M.

Zoey starts talking.

6:04 P.M.

Aisha arrives in Weymouth station and greets Christopher. One witness to the greeting is heard to say, "Good heavens!" in a very startled way.

6:15 P.M.

Julius calls Nina at the Grays'.

Nina calls the phone company is an attempt to have both her own and the Grays' number changed.

7:00 P.M.

Fearing laryngitis, Zoey pushes Nina out the door.

7:01 P.M.

Zoey begins fifth draft of dedication speech.

7:45 P.M.

Lucas comes to pick Zoey up and take her to the Historical Society.

"Zoey, your hands are like ice," Lucas said, trying to lace his fingers through hers.

"I can't help it," she moaned. "I'm so nervous. I was sweating so badly a minute ago that I soaked a big hole in my speech." She held up the ragged piece of paper to show him.

"What's to be nervous about?" Lucas asked.

"Um, other than the fact that I finished my speech about four minutes ago?" Zoey said. "And—"

"Hi, Zoey."

She turned. It was Aisha, looking prettier and more radiant than Zoey had ever seen her and holding hands with Christopher.

"Oh, my God!" Zoey said, throwing her arms around Aisha. "What are you doing here? Don't tell me you came all this way for my speech because I can tell you right now that you'll be disappointed."

"Oh, no, I just came to see Christopher," Aisha said. "But I'm sure your speech will be great."

Lucas frowned. "I thought you just went to Boston last weekend," he said to Christopher.

Aisha and Christopher exchanged a long glance. "He did," Aisha said finally. "But there was some stuff we hadn't resolved."

Zoey guessed by the look of them that they had resolved it.

"Come on, Eesh," Christopher said, pulling her away gently. "Let's get some punch. Good luck, Zoey."

Aisha gave her a small wave, and Zoey nodded. She watched them go.

"What are you looking at?" Lucas asked.

"Oh, I don't know," Zoey said. "They just look so . . ."

"Happy?" Lucas suggested, and when Zoey turned and saw the look in his eyes, she caught her breath, and for that instant she wasn't nervous at all.

Claire caught Nina's arm as soon as she came in the building. "Where have you been?" she demanded.

Nina gave her a sour look. "I had to walk, having been forbidden to drive the car again in this lifetime. And then I circled the building a bunch of times to make sure Julius McMartin wasn't hanging around."

Paolo showed up and gave Claire a cup of punch.

"Hi, Nina," he said. "Some guy just offered me twenty bucks for your phone number."

163

"Not Julius," Nina moaned. "He is here after all."

"Little guy?" Paolo asked. "Looks like he's probably good at math?"

"That's him," Nina said.

"Who?" Benjamin asked, appearing at her elbow.

"This guy who wants Nina's phone number," Paolo said.

Benjamin's face darkened. "Why does he want your phone number?" he asked Nina.

"To ask her out, obviously," Claire said quickly. "He's incredibly handsome."

Benjamin scowled.

"Hi, Mrs. Passmore!" Claire said, looking beyond Benjamin. "It's nice to see you. I didn't realize you were out of the hospital. Hi, Mr. Passmore."

"I just got out tonight," Mrs. Passmore said. "Benjamin picked me up and brought me here for Zoey's speech."

Claire introduced Paolo to Mr. and Mrs. Passmore before the Passmores moved off to find seats, Benjamin glancing back worriedly.

"Thanks a lot for telling Benjamin that Julius is handsome," Nina said sarcastically. "That's probably the biggest lie ever told in a public building."

"What's wrong with you?" Claire asked. "Benjamin looked like he wanted to challenge Julius to a duel."

Nina yelped. "Good God. That's just what I need."

"Hey, there's Zoey," Claire said. "Wow, she looks so pretty."

Both Paolo and Nina stared at her.

"What?" Claire asked. "It's not like I never say anything nice, is it?" She laughed. "Don't answer that!"

Her footsteps sounded very loud to Zoey as she crossed the floor to the podium. *Don't trip,* she told herself. *Just keep walking, one foot in front of the other.*

She reached the podium, arranged her speech carefully in front of her, looked up at the expectant faces—and that's when she knew she couldn't do it.

I can't read this speech, she thought, panic rising. *It's not what I want to say. I'm going to have to tell all these people that my speech isn't good enough. I'm going to have to bow out—*

She swallowed, and the microphone dutifully picked up the loud click in her throat. Zoey put a hand to her neck and tried to smile out at the sea of faces.

One of them was smiling back.

She squinted.

Mom? she wondered. *What's she doing here?* But her mother was definitely there, sitting between her father and Benjamin. Zoey's eyes filled with tears, and she smiled even wider.

The silence grew longer.

Zoey cleared her throat.

"I'm sorry," she said in a strange, unnaturally calm voice. "I had a speech prepared, but I don't think I can read it."

A slight ripple passed through the audience. Zoey found her mother's face again.

"I had written a speech," she said again. "But now that I'm standing up here, I think it would be best if I just repeated something that Carlos Ruggles, bosun on the *Carolina,* said to me last night. I think you'll agree that he said it much better than I ever could."

at the audience again.
...o dedicate this to the crew of
...n those who perished and those
...d . . . and to anyone who has known
...g and shown bravery."

She looked at her father, and he nodded. *He knows I mean Lara,* Zoey said. *Even if I didn't say her name.*

She closed her eyes, bowed her head slightly, and began repeating Mr. Ruggles's words.

"It only took the rescue ship seven minutes to reach us," Zoey said, "and in that time thirty-two men died in the subzero water."

She hadn't memorized Mr. Ruggles's words, and they came back slowly to her. She had to stop often and wait for the rest of a sentence to come to her, but the pauses only made her words more powerful, and by the end the whole audience was crying . . . and clapping.

Oh, that was great! Nina thought, getting to her feet and cheering along with everyone else. *Oh, Zoey, how perfect!*

As though hearing her name called, Zoey suddenly sought Nina's eyes. Nina smiled and gave her a thumbs-up sign, and Zoey broke into the most pleased grin Nina had ever seen.

She cares what I think! Nina thought, still clapping. *She cares because she loves me.*

And suddenly it seemed to Nina that love was everywhere in the Historical Society that night.

Love was as sweet as the glance between Nina and Zoey, bright as the air between Aisha and Christopher, hot as the sparks between Claire and Paolo, proud as the way Mr. Passmore was looking at Zoey, fierce as (yikes!) the way Julius McMartin was looking at Nina, satisfying as the jealousy on Benjamin's face, passionate as Lucas's feelings for Zoey and bigger . . . oh, much bigger than the mistake that had driven them apart.

"Oh," Nina said breathlessly. "Aren't we lucky?"

"Nope," Paolo answered. He reached for Claire's hand. "Luck had nothing to do with it."

MAKING OUT

by KATHERINE APPLEGATE

Available wherever books are sold.

MAK 0900